Moonbeam

By

Giovanni Andreazzi

authorHOUSE™

1663 LIBERTY DRIVE, SUITE 200
BLOOMINGTON, INDIANA 47403
(800) 839-8640
WWW.AUTHORHOUSE.COM

First published by AuthorHouse 10/15/04

ISBN: 1-4184-8251-X (sc)
ISBN: 1-4184-8252-8 (dj)

Library of Congress Control Number: 2004097337

Printed in the United States of America
Bloomington, Indiana

This book is printed on acid-free paper.

Dedication

This book is dedicated to my parents, who took the brunt of my growing up. They worked hard to provide a home, clothes, food, and their own version of love that nourished me and my sisters to make us what we are today. I inherited their genes, good and bad, and am trying to make them proud, even if they are not here to witness the attempt. So to you, Mom and Dad, I dedicate this story.

Acknowledgments

I would like to thank Barbara Tulloch, a friend and ex-coworker, who was my "Ideal Reader" for this book. She read, corrected errors, made suggestions, and provided encouragement on the final draft.

Also, thanks to George Brady, who was a constant companion growing up in our hometown, and is now a true friend growing older in the world. He is Boo in the story.

I would also like to thank Bobbie-Lou for providing the inspiration for the love story contained here in.

The other minor players, David and Skubini, are also real friends. They are both wonderful people, and I ask their forgiveness for the liberties I have taken with their childhood characters.

There are many others to thank, but I have looked at other acknowledgment pages by other authors, and if they seemed long, I did not read them. So for the sake of brevity and to allow you, the reader, to get to the story sooner, I only thank one more person and that is you.

Prologue

Some of the events in this book actually took place; however, I have taken writer's privilege in expanding and modifying them to fit the story.

I have worked with Native Americans in helping them build, maintain, and repair health, housing, and educational facilities on various reservations throughout the country. I found the conditions of some of the structures deplorable and unacceptable by modern standards. These are the same facilities that, by various treaties, our government is sworn to maintain. American natives were forced by those who preceded us to move and live on reservations, but that does not relieve us of our duties to uphold what was promised them. I am not a spokesperson for them. I am only trying to show the atrocities done in the past in hopes that we do not repeat them in the present. For more information on the massacres depicted in this book, you can find them on the World Wide Web in several locations using a search engine.

I grew up in a small town in Ohio. The name of the town is not important. It was like all small towns with a population of close to 30,000. There was a lot of heavy industry on the north end, with Main Street (downtown) close by. The houses at the newer end of town, two miles south of downtown, were built at the end of World War II. That is where the characters in this story all lived. There were several elementary schools, two junior high schools, and one high school. There was only one Catholic Church, with a Catholic grade school. Other churches abounded, but to me, they were all classified as Protestant. For a small town, there were a lot of public parks, which were a magnet for us when we were not in school. There was also a college, which provided substitute teachers for some of our classes. All characters in this book lived on Watson Avenue. Silver Park was a block away and was the nicest of the town parks.

Most of the shops were downtown; however, there were neighborhood groceries and drugstores near Watson. State Street, considered the second downtown, was two blocks north of Watson, where other shops also started to pop up. State Street soon attracted more shops, and the original downtown vanished. State Street was also located in the "better" part of town. The Strand movie theater was in the downtown area. The Mount Union Theater was a block north of State Street.

A train station was located in the downtown area. There was a rail line that ran three blocks west of Watson.

Table of Contents

One

I can remember the year as 1955. We had a new green and white 1954 Dodge station wagon that my dad got right after the new ones came out the September before. It was also the summer Boo and I killed all the birds in the Watson Woods, or at least attempted to. I had my first BB gun, a Daisy Red Ryder carbine with the Red Ryder's signature engraved on the stock. I bought it from Dave with the money I earned cutting grass. Boo had his Red Rider for a while, so he was the better shot, but I soon caught up with him in the accuracy department. We always coveted the headshot, and I had the only in-one-eye-and-out-the-other shot of a robin perched on a branch. I will never forget the sight as the murdered bird swung upside down, still clinging to the branch with both feet. It finally dropped to the ground with a hole clean through its head where its eyes had been. I am not proud of the fact that the two of us nearly wiped out the bird population in one day, nor will I forget the birds all lined up on the ground by mid-afternoon. After all, we were just ten- and eleven-year-old boys with BB guns.

I was called Andy, which was a shortening of my last name. Boo was his baby cousin's pronunciation of his nickname, Butch. His real name was George, but I never heard anyone, other than a policeman, call him that. That summer we were almost inseparable and we still keep in contact every other year or so. When the bird population was down to nothing, we started to shoot at each other in a hide-and-go-seek sort of way. That came to a halt when Boo shot my hat off when I peeked out from behind a large tree. The BB grazed my head, and, remembering the dreaded "you'll shoot your eye out" from my mother when I told her I was buying a BB gun, I told Boo we needed to stop. Our next target were the many field mice that we coerced out into the open with bits of bread while we hid in a refrigerator box with small aiming slits cut in the sides. The mice soon disappeared too, so we had to turn to some other sport.

The Watson Woods was an undeveloped piece of property between Watson and Cherry Avenues. At its widest it was probably 500 feet, but its length was the entire block from Mill to Milton, which was soon shortened by Catherine Lane. So I guess we had about ten to fifteen acres to patrol and play in. A drainage ditch emerged in the middle and ran south through the north half of the woods. It cut a steep slope on the east side (our side) and a gradual slope on the west (Pinky's side). The south half of the property, without the drainage ditch, was fairly flat. The entire acreage was full of locust, black walnut, maple, apple, and various other trees. Where the trees were sparse, underbrush and thorny blackberries covered the ground. Water ran continuously from natural springs and combined with the runoff from Cherry Avenue.

My first recollection as a person occurred at the fringe of the woods. To keep us out of his yard, Mr. Kessina built my sisters and me a swing set out of trees, boards, and ropes. I remember sitting on the swings, when David came over to play one afternoon. I knew he was old enough to go to school. I would start kindergarten next year, so I was home playing alone.

"Why aren't you in school?" I remember asking.

"It's only half a day," he said. I must have been four years old, but I remember the conversation clearly.

The Watson Woods are no more, having succumbed to the expansion of a nursing home infringing east to west from Cherry Avenue. The north side still has some of the original topography, but the fort I'm sure is gone. The fort was where we had the strangest experience of our lives, or anyone's for that matter.

Boo was a year younger than I, but a whole lot older in terms of boldness. We were about the same average-for-our-age height, but he culminated in a jet-black burr haircut, while I was topped with a blond flattop. I wore glasses, the kind with the thick, plastic frames. I had them since the third grade. My parents thought I needed them when they noticed my eyes watering while watching "Uncle Miltie" on TV. Although I was supposed to wear them all the time, I only wore them while secluded in the privacy of home doing homework or watching TV. Being farsighted, I got away without wearing glasses all the time, until I got my first pair of contact lenses in 1968. At eleven years old, I could also read without the glasses. My parents thought I needed glasses, so to appease them, I put them on when I watched TV or did my homework.

Boo was of slight build, but I was a chubby, healthy Italian boy. My Italian mother loaded my plate at every meal. She also loaded my sister's, who discretely shoveled what she did not want or could not eat onto my plate. My parents could not understand why I kept getting heavier while my sister looked anemic. To help me lose weight, they put me on skim milk. That didn't work. If I had not played so hard in the woods with Boo, I would have been even heavier.

After we annihilated all the birds, shot each other up, and killed all the stupid mice, we decided to dig the fort. We had attempted to dig forts before, but they were not very impressive. This time, however, we were determined to build the best and biggest fort ever. The site was carefully chosen, which was the side of the hill, on the steeper east bank of the ditch. The site was near the crest of the hill protected by thorny blackberry bushes and other dense undergrowth. Our first task was to cut a pathway to the fort's entrance about halfway down the slope from a not-too-steep existing path. We used folding army shovels that doubled as pickaxes. The dirt was neither too hard nor too rocky, so we completed the pathway in one day.

The next morning we set about digging into the side of the hill. The hill was caving in on us, which was not unexpected. To shore it up we cut down some small locust trees with hatchets and laid them crossways on the roof of the fort. We then covered them with an old canvas tarp we found, and buried the whole top with dirt from the dig. Candles in shelves dug out of the sides illuminated our work. It took the better part of the week to complete the dig. When we were done, it was about eight feet wide, fifteen feet deep, and four feet high.

On the last day of excavation, while we were moving in two lawn chairs, which we never unfolded, and a cable spool, to serve as a table, dirt crumbled away from the back wall, partially exposing some bones. They were large bones that we thought must have been someone's dog or maybe a bear that had died many years ago. There were three of them, the longest of which was seventeen or eighteen inches long and about an inch thick. The other two were about one inch long and the thickness of a pencil. We decided not to dig them completely out, and left them exposed like an artwork relief. I must admit it gave the fort a spooky look.

We did not do anymore to the fort over the weekend, partly because it rained Saturday. Sunday I had to go to church and then my grandmother's house for dinner. We always called lunch dinner and dinner supper. Boo's grandmother lived with them. He did not go to church, which made me somewhat jealous, but his family did have a family get-together on Sunday afternoons.

Boo and I took up a habit we copied from our parents. Both of his parents smoked and my dad did too, although my mother abstained. We would either sneak cigarettes from our parents or swipe them from the corner store. My dad had a roll-your-own machine, so it was easy to make a few and sneak them out of the house. My dad smoked unfiltered Camels, and Boo's parents smoked unfiltered Chesterfields, both strong brands. So, for a milder filtered brand, the corner store was a favorite place to swipe a pack or two. On rainy days, the owner of the store would let us sit on the floor near the main entrance to fold the papers for Boo's paper route. The cigarettes were in an open display case adjacent to where we sat folding and stuffing newspapers into canvas bags. In with the folded papers, would also go a pack or two of whatever was available on the adjacent shelves. Because of the cowboy ads on TV, our favorite was Marlboro. Sometimes a candy bar would find its place by the stolen cigarettes as well.

Although I say we smoked, we did not inhale. I did not find out that you were supposed to inhale until the next summer when my dad found out we were playing adults with a smoking habit. He made me sit in the basement and smoke a cigar. When he saw I wasn't inhaling he told me to breathe it into my lungs. I thought my lungs were on fire when I did this and never touched a cigarette again until I was in the navy. I guess he did not consider the fact that our whole family was exposed to second-hand smoke from him as long as we lived there.

It quit raining Sunday afternoon, so that night was our first night to sleep out in the fort. We talked, sitting cross-legged on our sleeping bags that were spread out on the dirt floor. We had a small campfire going near the opening to keep any wild animals from attacking us in our sleep. There weren't any wild animals in the Watson Woods, but it was fun to pretend. It did not occur to us that the fire partially blocked our only way out, but what the heck, we were just kids. Carefully laid beside our sleeping bags were our trusty BB guns.

We were having a cigarette, waiting for the crackling fire to cook the potatoes we placed in tin cans at its base. I don't know where we got this idea, maybe from one of the Hopalong Cassidy episodes on TV, but we never did it again. The potatoes cooked all right, but they had a charcoal crust on them that was inedible. There wasn't much left on the inside to eat and we didn't have anything to put on them, which made them very dry. We read comic books a lot for entertainment, so we must have read ourselves to sleep that first night by the light of the campfire. The fire cast our shadows, which danced eerily against the bones imbedded in the dirt at the rear of the fort.

The next thing I knew, I was awakened by the smell of tobacco smoke sometime in the night. "Boo, are you smoking?" I asked, looking around to see if there was a glow from the end of his cigarette.

"No, it is not your friend," came a deep voice I did not recognize. I immediately thought I must be dreaming and decided to curl back up in my bag, until I saw a movement near the rear of the cave. The fire was still smoldering, but offered little in the way of light to the inside of the fort.

"Are you Pinky?" I asked. Pinky was the scourge of Cherry Avenue. He had destroyed our other, smaller forts as soon as he discovered them. He was two or three years older and mean as hell. He had an Elmer Fudd speech impediment, and hated being reminded of it. Boo and I came across him and his friends one time in the woods. Before they knew we were there, we heard him say, "Wook, guys, I fwound a twee." When we mimicked him, we were chased down and received a beating. After that, we steered clear of him and his buddy Gary.

Pinky was also not the ripest apple on the tree. One story I heard was that he took the advice of a substitute teacher literally. The teacher told him, when he forgot a homework assignment, to make a note and put it where it could be found, like "in your ear." The rest of the class knew this was an obvious joke. A trip to the hospital the next day to remove the rolled-up note from one stupid student got the teacher in trouble, and Pinky the dunce of the year award.

Both Pinky and Gary were in a horrific automobile accident when they were just sixteen. Pinky was decapitated on Highway 62, when the Pontiac he was driving slammed into the rear of a truck that had lumber sticking five or six feet out the back. They were going in excess of 100 miles per hour, and after hitting the lumber, the Pontiac careened off the highway and came to an abrupt halt wrapped around a substantial, unyielding oak tree. After we heard about it, Boo and I rode our bikes to Briton's towing yard to see the car. It had no roof and was bent nearly in half. We also visited the tree, which had some bark removed but was otherwise undamaged. We never saw Gary again, and some say he was not altogether mentally right after holding Pinky's head in his lap—eyes staring up at him and bloody mouth gaping. With both of his legs pinned under the doubled-over dash, Gary held the silently screaming skull until they could get him out of what was left of the Pontiac. After terrorizing us most of our young lives, I guess he got what was coming to him.

"No, I am not a Pinky," was the reply. I could see the glow from the top of what looked like a pipe accompanied by the sound of someone breathing in. That was followed by the sound of someone softly exhaling through pursed lips. I knew the sound well because my grandfather smoked a pipe. This pipe seemed to be a lot longer and the odor was not the same as the pipe tobacco grandpa used.

"I took the liberty of unwrapping some of the tobacco from the paper you had on the table," the voice continued. "I hope you don't mind. It has been many years since I have had tobacco. I lit my pipe from the embers in the campfire."

"Are you the cops?" I asked, immediately regretting the choice of words. I thought he could be Mr. Sovero, our neighbor who was a policeman and also smoked a pipe. The voice did not fit, but the smoke he inhaled could have altered it.

"What is a cop?" he asked. By now I was getting curious, and slowly unzipped my sleeping bag and pulled the top back so I could get out. Boo was fast asleep in his bag, and if kids could snore, he would have been.

"You're kidding," I said as I sat up cross-legged on the bag, trying to focus toward the back wall where the voice was coming from. "A cop is a policeman."

"Then I am not a cop," he said, making the pipe glow again. From the dim glow, I could make out that he was naked, at least what I could see of him was. His hair was long and had a black sheen to it. I reached for my flashlight beside my comic book and flicked it on. The batteries were almost spent, and all that the bulb would produce was faint, orange glow.

"If you want to see who I am, put some more sticks on the fire and we can both get a good look. Don't be frightened by what you see. I am here as a friend in need of some help." I stretched

9

across my bag toward the fire, reaching for the sticks we gathered and laid beside the dirt wall the evening before. I took three of the larger ones and placed them over the embers in a tent-like fashion. I then placed some of the smaller ones directly on the embers and blew on them until they caught fire.

"Not a bad fire starter for a non-Indian," the man said. When the flames leapt to life I knew what he meant, for sitting cross-legged at the rear of the fort was what looked like someone from one of the cowboys and Indians movies Boo and I liked to go see at the Strand Theater on a Saturday afternoon. His jet-black hair reached halfway down his back. It was tied back by a piece of leather wrapped around his forehead. He was naked above the waist and wore buckskin pants tied at the waist with what looked like more rawhide. He was wearing plain, brown moccasins that were probably made from deerskin. He was holding a long pipe made out of what looked like carved wood. A thin wisp of smoke wafted upwards toward the exposed timbers of the ceiling. His eyes reflected the glow of the dancing fire like black marbles lit from within. Unlike the Indians in the matinees, he had no "war paint" on his face or body. Beside him were two cigarette papers stripped of their contents. "Thank you again for the tobacco. It helps me come back from beyond."

"Beyond what?" I asked with a screwed-up face. I understood as soon as he smiled exhaling through thin, pursed lips. I looked behind him to the rear wall and noticed gaping holes where the bones had been.

Teak-qwa Sung Anai-aqui was his native name, which translated roughly as The Catcher of Many Fish. He was the second son of Ite-na a-ween, one of the best hunters in the Unalactigo sub-tribe of the Lenni Lenape tribe, which originated around the lower Delaware River below what is now Philadelphia. During the late 1600s the tribe was forced to migrate west to get out of the way of the Dutch settlers. In 1780, when Teak-qua was a young warrior, the tribe was living in northeastern Ohio. While out hunting, it was his misfortune to be captured by Pennsylvania volunteers who mistook him for a member of the Moravian tribe. The Moravians angered the Pennsylvanians by stealing food from their storehouses. He was thrown in with ninety captured Moravians to be killed the next morning. During the night, he made a brave escape, but was wounded by a guard. The rest of the captured Moravian tribe was bludgeoned to death with wooden mallets. Teak-qwa, fatally wounded, wandered through the woods until he died. He was found by his tribe and given a burial at the site of our fort.

"I'm not believin' this shit," I said using one of the few swear words I understood the meaning of. I would confess the sin next Saturday so I could go to communion and not raise suspicion from my mother. "You're a dead Indian whose bones we found in the dirt back there?"

"Call me dead if you want, but my spirit lives. You freed me from the earth that kept me trapped for almost two hundred years."

"You've been dead for two hundred years?" I asked without wanting a response. I reached over and shook Boo, who just rolled

11

over and kept sleeping. "Boo, wake up, you ain't gonna believe this shit." I was up to three Hail Mary's and two Our Fathers at this point. After this night I would probably be up to a rosary and a stations of the cross. Boo did not stir.

"Leave him be," Teak-qua insisted. "I will speak to both of you in due time. I have some work I want you to do for all of my people."

"All of your people?" I said. "What do you mean?"

"For twenty years," Teak-qua began, "the white man pushed us farther and farther west from our lands. When we got this far, the soldiers with the red coats, asked for our help."

"The British?" I interrupted.

"They were the enemy of the Long Knives who pushed us west," he continued.

The squatters who fought the Indians before and the British during the Revolution must be the Long Knives. I thought, not wanting to interrupt him again. *This must have been right around 1776, before Ohio was part of the original thirteen states.*

"Other tribes, the Seneca, Mingo, and some of the Shawnee, attacked settlers on our lands. The Long Knives attacked my tribe, the Delaware, in retaliation, even though we had done no harm to the white man. Our chief, Koquethagachton, who the Long Knives called White Eyes, went to a place called Philadelphia and talked to the newly formed government."

He must be talking about the Continental Congress of 1776. This is my history class coming to life. We were never told the Indian's side of the story.

"Our chief was told there was nothing that could be done. They had no control of the Long Knives west of the mountains."

He must be referring to the Appalachians.

"Chief Cornstalk of the Shawnee was taken as a hostage and killed. His tribe retaliated in the lands east and south of the great river.

Must be the Ohio River. The land he is referring to must be Pennsylvania and Kentucky.

"The soldiers from a fort where the two rivers form the great river attacked two of my people's villages."

He's referring to Fort Pitt, where Pittsburgh is now. My dad has a friend from World War II there that we visited last summer.

"They were a peaceful people, but among those that the soldiers killed was the brother of the chief of the village clan. Also, they wounded his mother. The chief was going to retaliate, but the other two clans kept him calm. When the leaves were falling off the trees, all three clans went to the fort and signed a treaty. My people were promised our land would not be taken, we would be protected from the Red Coats, and we could be represented in their meetings in the place called Philadelphia."

This is incredible. Why weren't we taught this instead of memorizing all those dates and presidents' names?

"My people helped the soldiers in their war against the Red Coats, but did not fight. We were a peaceful people. My people and the Moravians became peaceful allies of the white man and the Red Coats. All we wanted to do was live in peace on our land. Instead, we were hunted down and killed. We could only survive by fleeing west. There are no descendants of my people alive today."

"What happened to you?" I asked, when he paused. After his relating all the bad things the white man did to his people, I was a little concerned for my own safety. My voice must have echoed the concern.

"You will find out soon enough. Do not worry," Teak-qua assured me. He had noticed my uneasiness. Even though I was second-generation Italian on my mother's side and third on my father's, I was a white man, and, as a race, just as guilty as the settlers. If Teak-qua turned hostile toward me, I could always point to Boo and say his ancestors could have participated, and therefore, were more culpable than I.

"Why are you telling me this?"

"You are here to help me and my people," he continued.

"Help you what?" was all I could think to say next as I squirmed a little closer to the fire and a way out.

Boo remained asleep as Teak-qua explained. "I can see that you are armed with weapons. Are you good with them?" I told him about the birds and mice, omitting the story where Boo almost put a permanent part in my scalp.

"But they are just BB guns," I offered.

"It does not matter," Teak-qua responded. "The fact that you are good shots and not afraid to kill is the important part. Can you ride a horse?"

"Yes," I said, not without some trepidation.

Boo and I both had ridden horses at a riding stable on the north side of town, and almost always with David and Skubini. Skubini was a nickname I gave him as a joke to make him sound Italian. We never knew David's ethnicity, so I never pinned a nickname on him. The White Horse riding stable, by the city cemetery, let us ride rented horses, escorted of course, along trails and an oval racetrack on their property. It was fifty cents an hour, and we could usually muster up an hour's worth of riding two or three times a summer. Riding our bikes the four miles to the stables, we would pick out the horse we wanted to ride from the "not too-spirited" ones. They looked enormous to us, but the trail leader/escort reassured us that they were gentle enough for little boys to ride. In most cases the escorts did not lie. Our first time, we were given some quick lessons on how to get on and off, how to guide, and how to stop the horse. Getting on and off the horse was the only part we really needed to practice, or so we thought, because we always followed the leader with the escort in front.

One time, my horse, a stallion named Blacky, was playing follow the leader until he came to a stream crossing. Apparently Blacky did not like the water, so instead of forging ahead with the pack, he held off until there was a clear shot to the opposite bank about ten feet away. My yelling "giddy up" was not working, until he decided it was time. With a mighty leap he made it to the other side. Had I not been holding on for dear life to the saddle horn, I would have landed ass first in the stream.

That same day, as we were following each other around the track, Boo had a fun experience with his horse. He was riding

Buttercup, a female who was touted as being very gentle. She was until she eyed a particularly enticing group of green grass in the center of the track. On the bike ride back to Watson Avenue, David, Skubini, and I laughed our asses off as we relived the sight of Boo galloping off into the middle of that field yelling, "Whoa, Buttercup! Whoa, Buttercup!" at the top of his lungs. The escort chased them on his horse until Buttercup came to the grass and abruptly stopped. Of course, Boo didn't, flying over the horse's bent down head, yelling, "Whoa, Buttercup!" So when I answered yes to Teak-qua's question, of the two of us, Boo was the only horse rider of record who was ever on a horse going faster than a trot.

"That is good," Teak-qua responded. "Because what I want you to do involves riding a horse a great distance."

"What if we don't want to help?" I asked yawning. My eyes were starting to droop as the fire was playing out and darkness was once again descending into the fort.

"You already have, my friend," Teak-qua said with a smile as I slipped into sleep. "You already have."

Two

The next morning, I told Boo about the Indian. We both looked at the back of the fort. The bones were right where they were the night before. Boo looked at me as if I was crazy and said that I had a bad dream from the potatoes we ate.

"You know, like in *A Christmas Carol*," Boo said referring to the movie we watched once a year, having never read the story. In those days, there were only two versions of the movie. Now there are 200.

"That was an underdone potato," I corrected. "The potatoes we had were overdone."

"So, I still think you're screwed up and lying 'cause you smoked two of my cigarettes when I was asleep," Boo responded, not having to worry about confession or stations of the cross. He used the word screw, although we didn't know what it meant. Our version of what screw meant, we learned later in life, was a perversion, not what the word really represented. We knew girls were not equipped the same as boys, but not until tenth-grade health class did we really learn about a girl's anatomy, and about periods. That was the same time I quit playing with those little white telescopes I found in the bathroom trashcan.

It was more awkward for Mr. Knowles, the tenth-grade health class teacher and football coach, to explain the female anatomy to a room full of eighth-grade boys, than it was for us to hear it. In college, Coach Knowles had been spiked in the eye playing football, so that both his eyes were not coordinated. Watching him nervously describe the female anatomy was an exercise in itself. One eye would look directly at you, while the other eye looked over your shoulder at the wall. Then the eyes would trade places. He reminded me of Jack Elam who played a drunk in *High Noon* and starred alongside Barbara Stanwyck and Ronald Reagan in *Cattle Queen of Montana*. Boo and I saw both movies at the Strand movie theater.

"Well, you slept through the whole damn thing," I said, mentally making the sign of the cross. "Tonight you stay awake with me while I try to summon the Indian. You'll see. He said he had a job for us with our BB guns and riding horses."

"What are we gonna do, chase down giant mouses and pop 'em?"

"It's mice," I said, always trying to correct my buddy. "I don't know what we have to do, but I think he said we already did it."

The rest of the day we spent at Silver Park, playing softball with other kids, some of whom were three or four years younger. We had a good team and won sometimes, but the fact that we had to play all the kids meant that the younger ones would keep us from winning against the good teams. We played softball at the park up to the time

I was going into my junior year in high school. That was the year after Mantle and Maris pulled the Yankees out of their slump. Boo and I batted back to back, and just like our Yankee counterparts, we used to follow each other with home runs. But that was a few years down the road. The day after the Indian introduced himself was the day Boo and I got thrown out of the park for killing a duck.

After we were done playing ball, we went for a bike ride on some of the steep hills in the park. Instead of riding two bikes, I rode on the handlebars of Boo's bike. That way we could go faster downhill, since I weighed more than Boo and the combined weight gave us pretty good momentum. The problem was that Boo could not see as well with me, blocking the scenery. So, when I yelled, "Duck! Duck!" he thought there was a branch in the way from the trees lining the railroad-tie path going down to the park duck pond. Instead, there was one of the park ducks waddling across the path directly in front of us. As Boo looked down to keep from getting whacked by a non-existent tree branch, he hit the brakes. The front wheel knocked the duck down, and the skidding rear wheel quite messily decapitated the duck, much like Pinky in the Pontiac (only that had not happened yet).

We could have gotten away with killing the duck if the park manager, the ubiquitous Mr. Kidwell, had not been ten feet away on an inspection tour. He was always in the park, since he lived in a house on park property. He was a large, barrel-chested man, who had an intimidating look. He always wore a wide-brimmed hat, partly because he was bald, but mainly to keep the sun off him during long hours outside making sure we kids didn't destroy his park. Most of the time he wore a dark shirt, dark pants, and a tie. This time, however, he was in blue-denim coveralls and a blue work shirt. He always had a walking cane with him.

Up until that time, I never saw a man as mad as he was. How he kept from killing us with that cane, I'll never know. Not only were we violating park rules by riding two on a bike, but we also decapitated one of his "pets" right in front of him. Had he not realized it was an accident, I think I would never have seen Teak-qua again. We were suspended from using park facilities for the rest of the summer, which meant we would be able to accommodate our Indian friend.

So, that night we retired to our fort. I anticipated the return of the Indian. Boo, mocking my comments from the night before by saying, "Wook, guys, I fwound an Indwian," made me wish I had not said a thing to him.

"When is your imaginary Indian gonna show up?" Boo asked. "I hope he doesn't interrupt my wet dream."

I had no idea want he meant be wet dream. I don't think he did either. He must have overheard the older boys talking about it and thought it was cool to imitate their language. I did not respond. I just stretched out on my sleeping bag, pulled out my Superman comic book, and started to read. Half an hour later, we were both asleep.

I awoke about two thirty to Teak-qua's chanting. To me it was soothing yet somehow sorrowful. He stopped the chanting long enough to take a drag on his pipe and to look at me with those shining, deep, black eyes.

"I see I have interrupted your dreams," he said. "I took some more of your tobacco. It is quite mild and burns very quickly." He set the smoldering pipe aside and resumed his chant.

"Help yourself," I said, rubbing my eyes. I grabbed Boo by the shoulders and shook him, calling for him to wake up. "Boo, Boo, wake up. Teak-qua's here."

Unlike the last time, Boo started to stir and mumble.

"Get me a cig," he said, squinting over to my side of the fort. "Who the hell's humming?"

"Teak-qua," I said. "And he ain't hummin', he's chanting."

"Yeah, damn straight," Boo said, turning toward the source of the noise. "Holy shit! There's an Indian in here," was Boo's response, as he squinted at the rear of the cave. "How the hell did he get in here?"

"I told ya, he was here," I said. "Those were his bones in the rear of the cave." I did a head gesture to the cavities where the bones had been, and would be again when the sun came up. I handed Boo his cigarette, while Teak-qua continued his chant.

"Does he talk?" was Boo's next response, as he bent to light the cigarette in the smoldering fire. This time we did not need to stoke the fire to light the fort. The full moon was setting in the west, casting a pale but adequate light in through the mouth of the fort and halfway back to where Teak-qua sat cross-legged. Teak-qua's hands were open and resting on the tops of his knees in a Yoga-like pose. His head was tilted back and his eyes closed. The chant emanated from his open mouth, but started deep in his throat, where his Adam's apple descended, and rose in rhythm to the change in tone. Neither

21

Boo nor I were willing to interrupt him. We just sat there staring, me unconsciously moving my mouth and Adam's apple in a silent mimic of Teak-qua, Boo sucking on the weed and turning his head to blow un-inhaled smoke toward the side wall of the fort.

Finally, Teak-qua stopped the chant and turned his head down toward us.

"You both are awake. Good, we can talk about your chores," Teak-qua said with a closed-lip smile. He picked up his long pipe and took the smoke deep into his lungs.

"Chores?" Boo and I said in unison.

"Call them what you may," he said, letting the smoke drift out with the words. "But, by destiny, you have work to do for me and my people. Listen to what I tell you. You have a long night ahead. Your first trip will be just to acquaint you with the distances you have to go and the changes you will encounter along the way. You will ride on Moonbeam—both of you. She will take you to your chores and bring you back again. She is a spirited horse, but gentle and strong. She will also protect you from any harm. She will always be near, watching over you and making sure you have what you need. However, you will not need much, and must take all your necessary tools with you. Make sure you have your guns with you when you travel on her. Other items must fit in your clothing or be held. Are you ready to begin your first trip?" He took another long pull on the pipe.

"Our guns are just BB guns, and where is this horse?" Boo asked. "How far are we going and will we be back for breakfast?"

"Your guns will be sufficient," Teak-qua answered, his voice mellowed by the exiting smoke. "Moonbeam awaits you in the place you call Silver, on an island in the middle of a pond. You will always return before the sun comes up, no matter how long the journey. Now go, and we will have more to talk about when you return." With this he set his pipe down and resumed the chants.

Boo and I just stared at each other in amazement. Finally I spoke.

"I guess we better get goin'. Looks like a nice night for a horse ride."

Boo said nothing as we stood and started out the fort entrance.

"Your guns," Teak-qua said, stopping the chanting long enough to speak.

"Oh yeah," Boo said as he retrieved both of our Daisys while I retrieved our sneakers.

We both shook the rifles simultaneously to make sure they were loaded with plenty of BBs. Hearing the reassuring rattle, we delayed just long enough to get into and tie our shoes.

I don't remember if we spoke all the way to Silver Park, the only place we knew with silver in its name and the only place we knew that had an island in the middle of a pond. We sneaked into the park as carefully as we could. We did not want to arouse the ire of Mr. Kidwell, especially when the duck's blood was still fresh on the wood path. As we approached the pond, we noticed all the ducks were on the side away from our approach. This was essential if we were to wade out to the island undetected.

We sat on the bank and took off our sneakers. We rolled up our jeans, tied the laces of our shoes together, and threw them over our shoulders. We knew the pond was not that deep on the side we were on. It was also the closest approach to the island. Almost every kid we knew had waded out to the island at one time or another, even though it was as forbidden as killing a duck.

The moon was casting a sheen on the murky water. The ripples from our slow fording were causing the reflection to dance on us and on the island ahead. The bottom of the pond was mucky from years of silt filtering in during heavy rains. Also, there must have been six inches of duck poop mixed in with the dirt. Each step was at the same time soothing and disgusting as the pudding-like bottom oozed between the toes.

"Shit, this water is cold as hell," Boo whispered.

I said nothing, but agreed with a shake of my head, although I wanted to correct him by reminding him hell is not cold. I also thought we would both be afforded the chance of finding out how cold or hot hell was, and soon, if Mr. Kidwell caught us.

When we got to the island, we laid our guns down, sat on rocks, and rinsed the mud from our feet in the pond water. We then gingerly slid our wet feet into our old sneakers. Next time, I was going to bring a dry pair of socks. We never wore socks in the summer, which meant for three months our feet were perpetually brown from the ankles up about two or three inches. We both stood up, picked up our rifles, and looked around for a horse. There were trees and bushes on the quarter-acre-sized island. The vegetation was dense enough that on the brightest day, the center of the island was hidden from view. On a moonlit night, we had to feel our way to the middle. We both had matches, but did not want to risk a light being seen by Mr. Kidwell.

"I don't see no damn horse," Boo whispered. "That Indian must have been crazy. Hell, we're crazy for comin' out here. I forgot my fags too."

"Here take mine," I said in response. "Let's keep looking. That horse has to be around here somewhere." I heard a chomp, chomp sound coming from over my right shoulder.

"What was that?" I asked as I turned in the direction of the sound.

"I didn't hear nothin'," Boo said.

"Let's look over here," I said, gesturing to the right with my rifle.

Boo followed, and as we moved closer to the edge of the island, we both stopped and stared. Our appreciation of horseflesh was limited to the swaybacked horses we rode at the stables and to those portrayed by Hollywood we saw on TV or at the theaters. We were never this close to a really magnificent mare. We knew it was a female because it lacked the large penis of the stallions we gawked at in the stables. The back of this horse was straight and came to the top of our heads. She was a honey color with a dark brown mane and tail. Her muscles were taut and rippled in the moonlight like the water we disturbed getting to the island. She must have sensed our presence, for she stopped pulling at the leaves on the bush in front of her and turned to look at us. If a horse could smile, she did. Her eyes were strangely light and multicolored. They looked like large

25

opals. It was as if she were a blonde goddess from the silver screen turned into a horse.

"Moonbeam," I whispered. I was rewarded with a nod from her head, her mane shaking like the hair on a Hollywood starlet striking a pose. If I could fall in love with a horse, this was the one. I could sense Boo getting the same signals as I.

"There ain't no saddle," Boo whispered. "What do we hold onto?"

"The first question is how do we get up on her back?" I shot back. As if sensing our predicament, Moonbeam turned toward us and bowed her head. She then put her nose down under my crotch and started to lift me up. Dropping my rifle, I grabbed her mane and in an instant slid down her neck as she lifted her head high. I found myself sitting on her, facing backward.

"Jesus," I said. I immediately made the sign of the cross, begging forgiveness. I then shimmied around so I was sitting on her facing the right way. She turned her head back and looked at me with those smiling eyes and nodded approvingly.

"Hand me our rifles," I told Boo. "Then gimmie your hand and I'll hoist you up."

The procedure worked, and we were now sitting on Moonbeam's back, wondering what to do next. I handed Boo his rifle.

"Giddyup," Boo said, grabbing the rifle from my outstretched arm.

"Oh caca," I said, grabbing Moonbeam's hair. Caca was an Italian word for shit. I sometimes said caca because, being a foreign word, using it was not a sin. After Boo said giddyup, I was bracing for the jolt like I got from riding Blacky at the stable. But a jolt did not come. Moonbeam turned forward and started toward the edge of the island and the pond.

"We're gonna get our shoes wet when she swims across the deep end of the pond," I said. But we did not get wet. When Moonbeam got to the water's edge, she started to trot, only it was like floating on air. Although I held on to her mane and Boo held on to the back of my shirt, we both could have let go. The ride was that smooth. She soon lifted us above the water, then the road, and then the trees. We were riding on a flying horse.

The trip was more like a rocket through a meteor shower. There were lights, but they streaked by in blurred ribbons. The only thing in focus was Moonbeam. I don't even know if Boo was in focus, because I was too shaken to turn around. I leaned forward and put my left arm around Moonbeam's neck, holding my rifle in my right arm and resting my left cheek against her mane. She smelled sweet, like honey, and not at all like the horses at the stable. Boo also leaned forward and found my back with his face, one arm around my waist. I could feel his rifle resting across the small of my back. I thought he might be sobbing. Moonbeam kept her legs working as if she were running on a track of cotton. I had heard the term "scared shitless," but until now, did not understand it. My butt was puckered so tightly, the worst case of amebic dysentery could not have separated the cheeks.

After what seemed like forever, Moonbeam slowed her feet, and the lights started to regain some shape. They could have been stars, but they were very big ones and very close. As quickly as the ride began, it came to an end. It was dawn in whatever world this was. The landscape started to take shape, only there wasn't much of a landscape. It was sand, sagebrush, saguaro and Jicarilla cacti, and a lot of other scruffy, low-growing plants. It was as if we were in an episode of the *Cisco Kid*, a Western we watched on Saturday morning TV. I wanted to turn to Boo and say, "Oooh, Pancho," and he would turn to me and say, "Oooh, Cisco," but when I turned back to look at him…. Something really strange had happened.

Boo wasn't a kid anymore. At least as far as size was concerned. Even sitting on Moonbeam he was at least a foot or more taller. His clothes stretched right along with his body. It was like looking at a distorted mirror in an amusement park. The look on his face must have mimicked my own, so I knew whatever happened to him, happened to me too. Our mutual distraction kept us from realizing we had stopped moving. Moonbeam let out a snort and bent down to nip at what little vegetation she could find. It was time to get down and shake off the disbelief we both felt. I swung my right leg over to the other side of Moonbeam and slid down. I didn't have far to go, and when I stood erect, I could see above Moonbeam's head. Boo followed suit, and we stood facing each other with open mouths.

"I am really gonna get the shit kicked outta me by my old man when I get back. If I get back," he corrected. "Hell, it's already morning."

"Teak-qua said we would get back before breakfast," I reminded him. "We have to trust him."

"And the horse," Boo added. Moonbeam snorted and shook her head up and down. That's when we noticed something else that had changed.

I looked at my Daisy BB gun, and Boo looked at his. They weren't Daisys anymore; they too had changed as we had. They looked like real guns, and when we shook them, there was no familiar rattle of BBs. They didn't rattle at all. We learned a couple of years later, from the movie *The Gun That Won the West*, that we were holding Winchester model 1873 carbines. They were fully loaded, and each of us had several bullets in each pocket. I made a mental note to bring along a pouch to carry the bullets or any other items that popped up in our pockets on our next trip, if there was a next trip.

"Shit, I wonder if these things really shoot," Boo said, not wanting a response. Not waiting for one either, he raised his rifle and took aim at the nearest saguaro. He pulled the trigger, just a second after I covered my ears. A loud report brought a jump and an angry whinny from Moonbeam. One arm of the cactus exploded from the impact. Boo's shoulder went back from the recoil, a bit more than he expected. After I uncovered my ears I noticed he was rubbing his shoulder.

"Damn, that hurt," he said. "I guess these things are real."

"I wonder what we're supposed to do with them," I added. "Teak-qua said this trip would be for us to get used to traveling."

"I think he said to acquaint us," Boo uncharacteristically corrected me.

"Well, let's have a look around," I said, ignoring his correction. I headed toward a small hill to our left, slinging the rifle over my shoulder, on its side, as a tired soldier would do. Boo followed, while Moonbeam returned to her grazing duties.

When we got to the top of the hill we both were looking down on a small town. Just like the surroundings, it looked as if we were in the middle of an Old West movie. I expected Audie Murphy to appear at any moment.

"Let's go down and look around," I said. "Maybe they're shooting a movie and we can watch." With that we started down the little knoll toward the town, about two miles away. Remembering Moonbeam, I turned to call to her, but she was already following about twenty feet behind. There was none of the characteristic clip-clop when she walked. I later discovered that she was unshod, and the lack of horseshoes made her steps soft and quiet.

Our walk to the town was uneventful, except when Boo had to piss. He stopped waving his gun around, drawing a bead on everything but Moonbeam and me.

"Man, I gotta piss," he said, as if this was a necessary announcement.

While he was pissing on the nearest pear-shaped cactus, I looked ahead and noticed movement in the town. It looked like there were men on horseback and women walking around. There were a few kids playing in the street. Off to the right were a couple of dust devils dancing on an invisible updraft of warm, desert air. Straight ahead in the distance was a mountain range. From the location of the rising sun, we must have been coming into the town from the southwest. It was a lot bigger looking the closer we got to the town limits. If this was made by Hollywood, it was on the scale of a set from *Samson and Delilah*, a movie that we saw at the Route 62 Drive-In five years earlier.

We just kept walking toward what looked like the south entrance to the town. As we got on the road leading into the town, there was a sign announcing we were entering Tucson. I scratched the short hair on the top of my head and said aloud, "Tucson. Tucson, Arizona? We came all the way to Tucson in one night? That can't be. This must be some type of dream we're havin', Boo."

We both stopped and stared at the sign. Moonbeam nudged me from behind with her nose, urging us to go on. She either was in a hurry, or wanted us to learn more. I believed it was a little of both. When we got into town, everyone we passed stared at us. I thought it might be that we were carrying rifles, but it looked like they were concerned about our clothes and especially our shoes. In addition to sneakers and Levis, we were both wearing T-shirts. Mine had a picture of Red Ryder and his sidekick, Little Beaver, with their names below each. Boo was wearing a T-shirt that claimed he went over Niagara Falls in a barrel. His was a lot newer than mine was, since his family went to the falls last summer for vacation. Mine was a least two years old and starting to stretch as I grew. However, the T-shirts, like the rest of our clothes, expanded with us, and, although a bad fit, they still fit. Moonbeam's head was bobbing up and down between us as she followed along. Those that weren't staring at us were looking at her.

"What time is it?" I asked the nearest man, who was dressed in a blue chambre shirt, chaps over a denim pair of pants, a dirty, brown ten-gallon cowboy hat, and boots that hadn't seen a shine, ever. He had a brown bandana around his neck, which could have been white at some time.

"Sunup," was his reply. "Nice lookin' piece of horseflesh. Wanna sell 'er?"

"No, thanks," I responded. "She's not ours to sell. She belongs to an Indian friend." I got a little nip on the back of my arm from Moonbeam as soon as I said this, indicating I was giving out more information than I needed to.

"You boys injuns?" he asked. Apparently we were not full-grown men, or at least looked like teenagers. "You don't dress like no Papagos. Don't talk like none neither. Your friend's horse ain't got no saddle neither, and ain't shod."

I restrained from correcting his double, triple, and quadruple negatives.

"Where's a restroom?" I asked, changing the subject. I did not want to whip it out like Boo did. Pissing on a cactus was probably a sin too.

"What da ya wanna rest from?" the cowboy asked. "There's a hotel down by the saloon."

"I need to go to the bathroom," I clarified.

"They got baths in some of the rooms," he said.

"No, I gotta take a leak," I said.

"Leak what?" he said with a quizzical look.

"He's gotta take a piss," Boo blurted out.

"That's behind the hotel," he said. "Or behind the general store, or behind any buildin', 'cept the jail house," he laughed.

"Thanks, Boo," I said. "Let's go."

"Well, do ya gotta piss or don't ya?" Boo asked.

"Let's just go," I said. "I think this guy is gettin' pissed himself."

"He kinda stunk a little bit too," Boo said, sotto voce. Moonbeam snorted as if in agreement. We continued down the dusty street looking for something, anything familiar. We stopped in front of a building that had a sheet of paper nailed to a post at the side of the door. I climbed the one step up and walked across the short, wooden walkway. What I saw almost made me piss my pants right in front of the building.

Boo noticed my surprise and walked over to where I stood with my mouth hanging open.

"What do you see?" Boo asked. And then he saw it too. It was a one-page newspaper with the date, "June 5, 1874," typed across the top. As we were standing there, a man came out of the building. He was dressed like the movie stereotype of a newspaper man from the 1800s: a hatband with a visor, some sort of pencil stuck behind his ear, white shirt with armbands holding up the bloused sleeves, and black pants. His hands were covered with black ink.

"Can I help you boys?" he said in a friendly voice.

"Y-yes," I stuttered. "What year is it?

"Eighteen seventy-four," he said without hesitation. "That's yesterday's news. I'm workin' on today's now. You boys can read?"

"Yeah, we can read," said Boo. "We just don't believe we're here."

"Where did you think you were?" he responded. "This is Tucson in Arizona Territory. You boys know how to write? If you do, I could offer you a job. I can pay each of you twenty-five cents every two weeks."

"No thanks," I said, not adding I could get three dollars in an hour cutting grass. "Let's go, Boo."

"Let's go over to the bar," Boo said, pointing to the building across the street.

I looked up and saw a sign reading, "Papa Joe's Emporium and Beer Hall."

"I don't know," I said. "We ain't old enough to drink."

"Bullshit," Boo said. "We grew a lot when we traveled here, and we look a lot older. I've got fifty cents too, and the sign says the beer cost a nickel."

"What do we do with Moonbeam?" I asked. "We can't tie her up. We don't have any rope."

"She seems to follow us wherever we go," Boo said.

I looked behind us and, sure enough, there was Moonbeam a few steps behind, watching our every move.

"Moonbeam, wait here," I instructed, as we stepped up on the wooden walkway. She seemed to understand and stopped short of the stair.

"I'll go in with you," I continued. "But I won't drink any beer."

"Suit yourself," Boo said, pushing open the double swinging doors.

We entered the bar and it wasn't much different than that portrayed by Hollywood, except it was a lot darker. The only light was from the door and open windows. It was a single, large room with a bar at the far end. There was a piano against the wall to our left, but there was no one playing. Tables on the right were unoccupied. The bar was almost empty. One really dirty looking man the size of a large black bear was leaning on the bar next to the windows by the tables. A slight breeze brought us the information that the man had not bathed in awhile. His body odor mixed with the smell of stale beer. A balding man in a white shirt with the sleeves rolled up, exposing the hairiest arms I had ever seen, looked up from his conversation with the dirty man.

"What can I do for you boys?" he said in a voice that sounded like he had a throat full of gravel. "We ain't open yet."

"Can I get a beer anyhow?" Boo asked. "He's got one." Boo pointed to the glass containing about an inch of amber liquid, sitting on the bar in front of the dirty man.

The dirty man turned to face us when Boo said that. I could barely make out the man's features. The light from the window behind him shadowed any part of his face not covered by his hat and a full, black beard. Even though I could not make out his eyes, I felt he was staring directly at me. A chill came over me.

"Maybe we better go," I whispered to Boo, who just kept advancing toward the bar.

"You got shit in your ears?" the dirty man asked. We all knew this was not a question. "The man said he ain't open."

The dirty man's voice sounded like a bear's grunt, deep and menacing.

"Don't start no trouble, Will," the bartender rasped out. "If they got the money, I can give 'em one beer. But then you gotta go." This last statement was, no doubt, directed at us.

"Now you're talkin'," Boo said. He put his elbows on the bar and he lifted his left foot to rest it on a rail, like we saw in the cowboy movies, only there was no rail. Boo's foot came down with a thump. He reached in his pocket and pulled out a cigarette and a pack of matches.

"Want one?" he said to the bartender, holding out the box of Marlboro's

"Them's strange looking cigarettes," the bartender observed. He reached out and took one from the flip-top box. "What the hell is this thing in the brown part on one end?"

Uh-oh, I thought. *These people have never seen a filtered cigarette, let alone a factory-made one.*

"It's the latest thing from back east," I said, thinking quickly.

"Here, you try it, Will," he said, tossing the cigarette to the dirty man.

The dirty man let it fall on the bar, reached over, picked it up, and ran it under his hairy nose.

"Don't smell too bad," he growled. He then pulled a match out of his vest pocket and ran the head of the match up his pants. The match burst into flames, and he lit the cigarette on the filter end.

"Damn, this tastes like shit," he said. He yanked the Marlboro out of his mouth and tossed it on the floor. "You can keep them screwed-up Yankee things." He then downed the rest of his beer to wash the taste out of his mouth.

The bartender was drawing a beer from the tap in the keg resting on the back counter as Boo pulled a quarter from his pocket and slapped it on the bar.

Just then I thought, *A quarter in 1874 is not going to look like the ones we have.*

I reached over and picked up the quarter. I almost shit myself, because I was holding an 1842 Seated Liberty quarter. I turned it over and there was the eagle holding an olive branch and arrows. Under the eagle was a letter O, indicating the quarter was made in New Orleans. Under that in a semicircle were the words "Quar. Dol." I turned it back over to get a better look at the seated Liberty. I noticed the date was in small letters.

"Damn," I said. I had only seen one of these in a book at the library. Boo and I collected coins, but all we could afford were pennies. We would buy circulated bags of pennies from the bank whenever we could afford it. We were always in search of the coveted 1909 SVDB. The S, indicating the San Francisco mint, was under the date on the front. VDB was the "wheaties," as we called them, designer's initials—Victor David Brenner—stamped on the back at the bottom. The earthquake limited production of the SVDB pennies, thus making them rare. We never found a 1909 SVDB penny, but every once in a while we came across and Indian Head cent. This quarter, though, was an unbelievable possession. As I ogled at the coin, it was snatched from my hand buy the bartender, just as soon he put down a beer in front of both of us. He looked at the quarter carefully, and then at me, probably thinking I had gone nuts.

"I-I-I didn't want a beer," I stammered.

"Well give it to your buddy then," the bartender said. He turned his back and put the quarter in a cigar box and pulled out two coins. Turning back around, he tossed the change on the counter. I was now staring at an 1874 Shield nickel in perfect condition and an 1874 Seated Liberty dime, also in perfect condition. I picked the nickel up and noticed a double-die stamp of the ring above the shield and under the arrow. I turned it over to look at the big 5 in the middle of thirteen stars. I carefully put the nickel down and turned my attention to the dime. There was nothing unusual about it, such as the double-die stamp on the nickel. Just the same, I had never held one, nor seen a picture of one in such good condition.

Boo took a drink of the beer in front of him. He almost choked when he put the beer down and swallowed. He then looked at me, wondering why my mouth was wide open.

"You got to try this shit," he said, in a not-too-loud voice. "It's warm and tastes terrible. I've had sips out of my dad's glass at home, but this is bad."

It was not that I was afraid to drink the beer; I too was introduced to alcohol at home. My dad let me sip his beer every once and awhile, and at Sunday dinner, my sisters and I were sometimes treated to a little bit of my grandfather's homemade table wine. I just did not want to drink and have the beer on my breath when we got back; anyway, I was preoccupied with the coins.

"You can have mine," I said back. "Look at these coins." I shoved them toward him. He picked them up and looked long and hard at them.

"Holy shit," he said.

"That ain't nothin'," I said. "This was change for a Seated Liberty quarter with a small date. The one you laid on the counter."

"It was an ordinary quarter when we left Ohio," he said. "It must have changed when we came here. Do you think these will revert to our coins when we go back home?" He was now staring straight ahead and thinking out loud, clutching the coins tightly.

"I don't know, but if they don't, we can get new bikes with what they're worth," I said.

"Let's go," Boo said. "I can't wait to see if they change when we get back home. I don't want anymore of this panther piss beer anyway." He put the coins in his pocket.

"Okay," I said.

"Well, we gotta run," Boo said to the bartender.

"What about your beers?" the bartender said.

"Hell, I'll drink them," the bear of dirty man said, making a move toward our beers.

We said nothing else as we left the bar. Moonbeam was out in the street waiting for us. We headed north on the street, shadowed by Moonbeam.

Once we got up the street past the next building, I told Boo we better think about getting on Moonbeam and heading back to the fort in Ohio.

"If this is real, it's gettin' kinda scary," I said. "If this is a dream, I wanna wake up soon." Boo nodded his head in agreement. Instead of walking all the way through town, we took the next alley to the right and worked our way between the second row of buildings. We found ourselves heading back into the desert. I pissed on a cactus, noticing my penis had grown too.

"We need to make a list of things to bring with us next time," I said. "One thing we need is a watch."

"What do you mean next time?" he responded. "We need to get back soon. I hate the thought of this being for real and we can't get back." We both looked at Moonbeam. She looked back with those large, opaline eyes.

"Can we head back now?" I asked Moonbeam. She gave a little whinny and shook her head up and down.

This time we mounted her from the left side. Boo made a foothold by cupping his hands together. Once he boosted me up, he handed me the rifles. We then locked left forearms, and Boo swung up behind me. Moonbeam turned to see if we were ready. When she was assured we were on and balanced, she turned her head and started to trot. As before, when she got airborne, the ribboned lightshow started. We glided through space, not saying a word. When the lightshow was over, we were approaching the island in the middle of the pond. It was still dark, but the moon had disappeared over the horizon.

Moonbeam pranced across the surface of the water and worked her way up onto the island to the center of the trees and shrubs. When we jumped down, we noticed we were our regular size. Our rifles rattled with BBs as they jostled with the impact of the jump. They were no longer Winchesters. As we walked toward the water's edge I looked around. Moonbeam was no longer there. We forded the pond as before and headed back to the fort. Our heads were hanging low, as we were both getting very tired. There was no Indian to greet us on our return, just some empty cigarette papers, the scent of tobacco smoke, and a barely smoldering fire. The bones were back in the wall. We both crawled into our sleeping bags and in less than a minute were fast asleep.

Three

When we woke up the next morning, we were strangely refreshed, as if we had slept straight through the night. Evidently, we had returned to about the same time as when we left. We started to laugh at what we thought must have been just a strange dream we both somehow had shared. When I reached in the pocket of my Levis and pulled out a .44-caliber bullet, the smiles disappeared like ice on a hot griddle. Boo suddenly remembered the two coins and reached in his pocket. He pulled out the coins and stared at them in disbelief. They were still 1874 vintage. He gave me the dime and put the more valuable nickel back in his pocket. As we walked to my house, our minds raced in third gear with questions to ask the Indian the next time we saw him.

After an okay from my mom, Boo and I headed to his house for breakfast. His mom was small in stature. She used to say she was small but mighty. At ten and eleven years old, our heads were at the same level as hers. Her jet-black hair was pulled back tight against her head. As with most of the mothers I knew, her face showed wear and tear far beyond her years. Also, like most of the mothers, she was always busy with laundry, cooking, sewing, cleaning, and taking care of her family. She would smack the back of the head of Boo, me, or any of the other neighborhood kids if we got out of line in her house. This was the same in any of our friends' houses. You either behaved or faced the consequences.

That morning she fried eggs. I never had eggs at home the way she cooked them. There was a lot of grease in the frying pan, so much that the eggs almost floated. After a few seconds of frying, she spooned hot grease over the eggs to cook the top. I didn't know grease was bad for your health until I got out of college and went on my first diet. I think I'm still carrying around some of that grease today.

As we finished our eggs and toast, Duane, or Skubini as I nicknamed him, was knocking on Boo's kitchen door. Skubini wanted to be our friend today. Usually, we only hung around in pairs, until one of us would pick a fight with the other and then we would pair up with someone else. A typical summer would pair me with Boo, Skubini with Dave, and then me with Skubini and Boo with Dave, etc. This was not a typical summer. Sometimes we all four would do things together such as riding horses or playing kickball in the street with the girls.

Skubini was Polish, I was Italian, Boo was Irish, and nobody knew what Dave was. Skubini's dad was the only white-collar worker we knew. All the rest of the dads came home dirty from work, and sometimes drunk. If they weren't drunk when they got home, a couple of beers would change that in a hurry. Skubini's family had money, or at least more than we did. Therefore, Skubini got a new, three-speed, English bike for Christmas, while the rest of us had to save paper route money or cut grass to buy our used Schwinn bicycles. We didn't resent this, as kids; we just accepted it.

Skubini went to Catholic school, where tuition was paid by the parents. We went to public school, which was paid for by taxes. So when Boo and I got arrested by the police on George Washington's birthday two years before, Skubini, who swiped the staple gun with us, was safely in Catholic school, which did not celebrate that holiday. Therefore, when we made up the lie in the police car the day we were arrested, we forgot to tell Skubini that we told the police our version of what happened to the stolen merchandise. So, when we went to juvenile court with our parents, and the judge blurted out the fact that we tossed the staple gun in the Silver Park pond, my mother threw a fit when she heard the judge. Our version was that we left it in a tree, and it was gone when we went back for it later. My court-assigned punishment of restriction to our backyard for two weeks was just the beginning. My parents punished me far worse than a mere backyard confinement.

Boo's parents were just glad it was only a staple gun. When the cop arrested us at Boo's house, the only person home at the time was his grandmother. She misunderstood and told Boo's mom we had stolen a gun.

Skubini was my age and about my height and weight. We both suffered from mothers who thought a healthy boy was a chubby one. Skubini had short, blond, curly hair, which was cut by a barber. My dad cut my hair until I went in the navy. Skubini had a dog named

Shotsie, which I think meant sweetheart in Polish; Shotsie could sit up and beg. Boo had a dog named Lucky that would chase us around the house until we threw up. Dave had a dog named Duke that we took for long walks on a choker chain. I had a chicken named PP, but only until he grew old enough to be "taken to the farm," as my dad said. PP had to be kept in a coop.

We told Skubini about Teak-qua and our trip to Tucson. We even showed him the bullet and coins. He was not going to believe us until he saw the bones, but our fort was secret. We were not going to take him there, so nothing more was said about it. I'm sure he thought we were telling a lie, just like we did with the disposition of the staple gun.

Despite our economic and ethnic differences, we all got along. That day, we would have all headed for the park to play ball, but because of the dead-duck ban on Boo and me, we needed to find something else to do. One game we played was blowing things up with firecrackers. Dave used to get firecrackers when he went to visit his cousins in Tennessee and then sell them to us. Today, we had none, and Dave was off doing something on his own, so we had to look for something else we could explode.

I don't know where we discovered calcium carbide. I know that carbide lamps were still used in the early fifties; I just don't know where, except maybe in the coal mines of western Pennsylvania. But somehow we discovered that if you put calcium carbide pellets in water, acetylene gas formed. We could buy the pellets at the local hardware store for less than a dollar. Kids could buy almost anything in the fifties as long as they had money, including cigarettes with a note from their parents. So, what should we do with the pellets? At first we put the pellets in a glass jar and poked holes in the metal lid. The idea was to throw the jar in water. The jar would sink, the gas would expand quickly, and the whole thing would explode. It only fizzed a lot.

We knew we could make the gas and that the gas would burn. Could we make it explode, and how could we? Next, we dug a hole a little larger than the tin can. We filled the hole with water, poked a hole in the top of a tin can, put pellets in the water, and put the can over the pellets. Gas started coming out of the top of the can, and Boo lit a match. He reached over to the hole with the lit match, and bang, the can nearly took his hand off as it rocketed out of sight. We heard the can come back to earth on someone's roof, somewhere in the neighborhood.

Not only did we lose our can, but we were also speckled with mud. Since we were behind Boo's garage, which was also speckled with mud, we decided we better take our carbide bomb-making laboratory to the safety of the woods. If Boo's mom had seen the mess we made, all three of us would have been smacked silly. We set off several of the bombs that day after re-designing the hole in the side of the can instead of the top. We also donned our yellow raincoats with matching hats to keep the mud splatter off our clothes, thus saving another smack or two. Turning our heads when lighting the gas also was learned from experimentation. Of course, the one who lit the gas could not see the can leave the pull of gravity, but the observers could by watching at a "safe" distance. The observers would also follow the can on its return to earth, so it could be retrieved for another launch. The cans lasted about three trips each before they were ripped at the seams and had to be replaced.

After Duane had gone home, Boo and I decided the carbide pellets were a "cool" thing to have on our next trip. Since fanny packs were not yet invented, we fashioned two canvas tote bags with a rawhide drawstring from scraps in my father's garage. We filled our tote bags with a can of carbide pellets, a pocketknife, dry socks, stolen candy bars, cigarettes, and matches. It was like a game of Dungeons and Dragons, only we had no name for it in the fifties. We took our bags to the fort that night along with Boo's Roy Rogers wristwatch with a genuine leather band. Above Roy's signature, on the face of the watch, was a circular picture of Roy and Trigger in the middle of a green background. I had in my pocket a watch I found in my dad's dresser, a forbidden place to go, that supposedly belonged to his father. It was a gold-plated pocket watch with a flip-up cover. It had a second hand, which the Roy Rogers watch did not. The Roy Rogers watch is worth five hundred dollars today, while my grandfather's is not worth a tenth of that.

We had a hard time falling asleep but eventually did. At twelve thirty, we both were awakened by a gentle nudge from Teak-qua. Boo rubbed his eyes and tilted his right arm toward the smoldering fire.

"It's twelve thirty," Boo announced, squinting.

"Be alert, my helpers," Teak-qua said. "It is time for your first task. This trip you will be gone for a short while, but longer than last night."

48

"How do you know how long we were gone?" I asked.

"Moonbeam is a special horse and messenger. She told me everything you did in my morning dream."

"Where were we last night?" Boo asked, reaching for and lighting a cigarette. "The sign said Tucson and the newspaper said 1874. Everyone was dressed funny and it looked like a movie set."

"You went back to a different time and place. Each trip will be to a different place. Each trip will be to a different time. However, each trip will be for the same purpose. You have freed me from the earth that bound me; now you must avenge my ancestors and my brothers. It is of no use to resist. I know that you have already accepted the tasks and performed them well, for I can also see the future as well as the past."

"Our guns changed, and so did we," I added to Boo's observations. I lit a cigarette of my own. "The guns had real bullets, and we were bigger."

"You need to have real guns, and you need to be bigger and stronger," Teak-qua said. "The tasks you are about to perform require both. You would not be able to do what is necessary as small boys. Did you not return in good health and the same as when you left?"

"We did, but I still had a bullet in my pocket," I said, "and Boo had some money that stayed old."

"The bullet was to make you believers. The coin was a gift as well as to make you believe. Without your souvenirs, you would have thought it was all a dream. I see you have a pouch to take items with you. Some of those items may change too. From now

49

on most everything you need must be on you when you arrive with Moonbeam."

"Why don't you do these tasks?" Boo asked. I nodded my head in agreement.

"Once I have died, I cannot go back or forward. I am forever trapped in the ground where I lie. Where I am sending you is no place for an Indian. Only a white man can mix with his own kind and is able to do what you are about to do.

"Enough questions for one night. You must go do your first task. Each time you go, you will be shown what the white man has done to deserve the punishment you will inflict. Seeing what they did will allow you to make sure your vengeance is not taken on innocent people. You will know who the guilty ones are without my telling you. Moonbeam awaits you in a field at the south end of the place you call silver."

"Are we going to have to kill people?" I asked. "'Cause that's a sin. I can't do that."

"Oh Jesus Christ on a crutch!" exclaimed Boo. "Those damn sins of yours. I'll waste the bastards. You can just turn your head."

"I think it's a sin to just be there while you do it," I said, making the sign of the cross over my heart. I looked back for reassurance from Teak-qua, but he was gone.

"Oh screw you, let's just go. Maybe we ought to stop and get your Jesus beads on the way to the park."

"Last night you didn't even want to go, and now you're anxious as hell. And it's a rosary, not Jesus beads." I was talking to the soles of Boo's shoes as he crawled out of the fort. I followed after him.

"At least we don't have to wade in the water," Boo said, as we left the Watson Woods.

"So much for bringing dry socks," I responded.

"It's almost one o'clock now," Boo said, looking at Roy and Trigger in the bright moonlight.

Imitating last night, the moon gave a platinum patina to all surfaces and pushed our short, faint shadows ahead of us. This time we skirted the Watson Avenue entrance to the park and walked south on Union Avenue. The main and southernmost entrances to the park were accessed from Union Avenue, one street west of Watson. This lessened the chance of encountering the dreaded Kidwell, even if it was after one in the morning. We had to go to the southernmost entrance to get access to the field where, we guessed, Teak-qua said that Moonbeam would be.

We knew the field well because there were other horses there. We used to pick undersized apples from the one gnarled apple tree in the Watson Woods and take them to the horses. Once, the owner of the horses came out and talked to us, offering to let us ride the horses anytime we wanted. We never took her up on it, but continued to give the horses apples, or anything else we had. Boo even gave one five pieces of bubble gum. We came back later to see if the horse had blown bubbles out of its butt. We had hoped to see a ring of gum around its poop chute like we had on our face when a bubble burst. To our disappointment there were no rings. The horse could have died from "rim-pucker-roo" for all we know (rim-pucker-roo was our medical term for a made up disease. If you had the rim, your butt developed red circles around it from eating strange food, and you can't poop. Sooner or later, you swelled up until you exploded).

As we skirted the locked, automobile entrance gates, we could see the field ahead and to the right. There was a substantial barbed-wire fence separating the field from the park. Even before we could see her outline, Moonbeam's eyes reflected the moon like two pearl buttons. It was like a beacon we could not miss, nor did we want to. Later in life when I was attracted to a woman, I would first look into her eyes to see if Moonbeam had somehow been reincarnated. I never found her.

Moonbeam seemed glad to see us. She let out a snort and shook her head up and down. Her mane waved in unison. We were able to stoop under the top line of barbed wire and step over the second line to gain access to the field. It was then that I noticed we had left the rifles back at the fort. We had the tote bag of items, but not the rifles.

"Should we go back and get the guns?" I asked Boo.

"Naw," he said. "Let's see what we can do without them."

"Yeah, maybe you're right." This time I made a step out of my interlaced fingers and let Boo get on Moonbeam first. Even though we were not as big as when we returned the night before, this procedure seemed to work well. He then reached down, and with the same left arm forearm lock, I pulled myself up behind Boo. I held the tote bag on Moonbeam's back between us. I was not going to leave it behind. I made a mental note to bring an apple for Moonbeam next trip. Not a shriveled up one, but a good one from David's backyard tree. She might like one of the candy bars, but I did not want her to get rim-pucker-roo.

"Giddyup," Boo said. We both knew this was unnecessary, but Boo just liked to say it. Moonbeam started her trot and then a gallop across the grassy field. We lifted up and cleared the fence and then the trees. This time, Boo and I were sitting tall in the saddle, a real figure of speech, since there was no saddle. We watched as the ribbons of light seemed to come from infinity, streak around either side of us, and then disappear into darkness behind us. It was like swimming through a sea of white-hot coals, but so fast you never touched them. Boo was not holding Moonbeam's mane, and I was not holding on to Boo. It was as if we were gliding on a cloud shaped like a horse, through time and space.

When Moonbeam came to a stop, we were in a lush forest, surrounded by trees in full autumn foliage. There was the sound of a brook nearby, unseen because of the dense undergrowth. The trees were familiar to us. There were oaks, maples, birches, and ash. They were tall and skinny from their hurried growth to get to the sun before the other trees blocked the precious light. The tote bag had turned into a saddlebag. Just like the first time, we were big again. We stayed on Moonbeam while she made her way through the woods along a deer path. After a short ride, we came upon an opening where an abandoned cornfield was bathed in the morning sun. Corn could be seen sticking out on the sides of the dried, yellow stalks. Moonbeam stopped and we stayed on her back, surveying the area and taking in the beauty of the pristine farmland.

"My watch says it's still one o'clock," Boo said.

"Mine ain't workin'," I said. "The second hand is stopped. My dad is gonna kill me if he finds out I broke his dad's watch." His dad was not the person I called grandpa. My dad's father beat on my grandma one too many times and she divorced him. When she remarried, she became a Methodist, since the divorce made her a bad Catholic in the eyes of the church. I never met my dad's father, so he was always my dad's dad. I called my dad's stepfather Grandpa.

A little while later, a group of Indians, men, women, and children, appeared in the field and began to gather what was left of the corn. We watched as they filled their baskets. Boo and I got off Moonbeam and sat against the trees, watching history unfold.

"Damn," Boo said as he checked to see what Roy was up to. "My watch must not be working either. It's still one o'clock.

I rechecked my chronometer to see if by some miracle it had fixed itself.

"Mine still says one also, but the second hand has moved a little bit," I said.

We both resumed our distant spying on the foraging Indians. As they were completing their task, the sound of men on horseback came from the right side of the field. The Indians heard it too and stopped gathering corn. Into the clearing marched a large group of men, maybe a hundred and fifty or more, some in uniforms, some in baggy pants and shirts, some on horses, some walking, all carrying muskets. They surrounded the group of ninety or so Indians and shouted orders we could not make out from our vantage point.

The group of Indians was made to march with the group of soldiers. One man in uniform was leading all of them. From the war movies and cowboy and Indian movies we had watched, we recognized the shoulder board, silver eagle insignia of a colonel. As they disappeared behind the trees along the dirt path, we followed. This must have been what Teak-qua meant by saying we will be shown what the white man has done, before we waste them. We followed all day, unseen, until they came to a group of buildings. By then it was getting dark. Our watches were still stuck on one o'clock. The second hand on mine had moved almost one complete revolution.

Moonbeam led us to a group of fallen trees, where we curled up, making a mattress and blankets out of bows of pine trees. Oddly enough, we felt neither cold, nor heat, nor hunger, nor did we want a cigarette. We just slept until Moonbeam nudged us awake at dawn.

"I got one thirty now," Boo whispered.

"I got one thirty too," I whispered back, after flipping up the gold colored cover of the watch I had. "But the second hand is not moving."

"I think I know what's happening," I continued, perking up. "The watches are on Ohio time. We spent the night here, but in reality, it's only been half an hour. That's how we manage to get back before morning.

"Wha'?" Boo asked, a little too loud. His face was tightened up like a fist.

"I don't know how else to explain it," I whispered. "Time is almost standing still for us. That's why we are never hungry when we go back in time. Our body clocks are not moving."

"But we get bigger," Boo countered. "Explain that, kemosabe."

"Teak-qua explained that last night," I reminded him. "We'll just have to accept his explanation." That ended the discussion, at least for now.

Both of us turned our attention to the job we were sent to do. We crept to the area just outside the buildings, where the soldiers and Indians set up camp the night before. Under the direction of the colonel, the Indians were led into one of the buildings. We did not see what happened inside, but we heard screams of terror and loud thudding noises. Boo and I cupped our hands over our ears to muffle the cries. After two seconds ticked off my watch, which must have been an hour here, men walked out of the building carrying bloody mallets. They were then led away by the colonel.

Without looking inside, we knew what had happened, but we needed to see anyway. We walked to the buildings with Moonbeam close behind. We peered into the open door. The morning light filtering in through the unglazed window openings and open door cast a dim light on the horror we witnessed. The bodies of the entire group of men, women, and children were lying in bloody heaps, some on top of each other. Their skulls were crushed; some of the faces were unrecognizable as human. There was no movement and nothing we could do but leave. Boo and I both gagged as we fell to our knees on the pine-carpeted earth outside the building.

Fortunately, we had empty stomachs, so nothing came up. We knew now what we had to do, but we had no weapons.

Moonbeam urged us along. Walking, we followed behind the murderers at a safe distance until we came upon small village. The murderers were lighting torches to burn all of the buildings. When we stopped, I went to the saddlebags draped across Moonbeam's back. I reached inside to see what time travel did to transform our treasures. I thought I had grabbed the can of carbide, but what I pulled from the bag was six long, red, flare-like sticks.

"Dynamite," Boo whispered. "We can blow them all to hell."

"Don't we need fuses?" I asked.

"Fuses, we don't need no stinking fuses," Boo said, mocking the Federales from the movie *Treasure of the Sierra Madres*. "We just throw them into the fire. Hell, from here it's just like tossing a softball from the outfield to home plate. The way they're all standing around watching the buildings burn, we can get quite a few of them. The colonel is right in front of us." There was no need to whisper now. The noise from the crackling flames and yelling men was getting quite loud.

"I'll take three of these around the other side, and you take the other three. When you hear the first explosion, toss yours. They'll be looking in my direction, so they won't see you lob one on a fire close to the colonel."

In what seemed like a couple of minutes, I was around the other side and tossed one of my sticks into the closest fire. It exploded immediately, laying out ten soldiers in one nasty blast. As

I was lobbing my second stick, I heard an explosion from the other side of the village. Screams could be heard all over, and soldiers were running in all directions. I threw my third stick into another building as my second one exploded. I started to run back to the other side when a fourth, fifth, and the final stick of dynamite went off. Before I could get to the other side, Moonbeam with Boo on her back came racing around the edge of the clearing. In one motion, I grabbed his forearm and swung up behind him. It was just like Roy Rogers snatching Pat Brady from his runaway Jeep Nellybelle in one of the TV episodes.

Moonbeam was up above the trees before we knew it. She circled around the village so we could survey the damage. There must have been sixty or seventy dead and dying murderers lying about the village. The colonel was kneeling, staring at his severed arm, watching the blood pumping out of an artery. As we got higher and started to move faster, he collapsed in his own blood, face down on his own severed arm. We both checked our watches and discovered it was two o'clock. We both let out our best "yeehaw" as the ribbons of light approached from infinity.

Up until now, the only other person I had seen die violently was a truck driver. Boo and I were riding our bikes one afternoon on an exceptionally warm winter day. We noticed a column of smoke in the distance north of town a few blocks away. Naturally, we took off riding as fast as we could in that direction. From two blocks away, we could tell this was no ordinary fire. Thick, black smoke was filling the air above a tanker truck in the middle of an intersection.

As we approached, the heat from the burning gasoline kept us half a block away. There were firemen trying to smother the heavy fire with foam. An ambulance waited a safe distance from the conflagration on the intersecting road opposite us. When the fire was almost under control, we could see what happened. A county snowplow, with its blade raised, ran a stop sign and, instead of snow, plowed into the Matlack truck full of fuel. The snowplow came to rest thirty feet away. The snowplow driver was sitting on the ground next to his truck, apparently unhurt. In fifteen minutes, the fire was under control.

When beckoned by the firemen, the ambulance moved in toward the tanker, and so did we. The closest we could get was fifty feet away in a frozen cornfield, adjacent to the driver's side of the tanker. We watched as the firemen pried open the soot-blackened, driver's side door while the medics wheeled over a gurney. Inside was a sight I will never forget. The driver's seated body was completely charred like a steak left too long on a barbecue grill. His arm was attached to the steering wheel as if he were still driving the truck. With the fireman's help, the medics tugged on the corpse's arm until it was yanked free. Then both of them dragged the body out of the cab and onto a gurney. The brown, plastic body bag under the body was then zipped up.

We watched until the ambulance headed back toward the hospital, its lights on, sirens off. We then turned and headed for home to tell the others what we witnessed.

Four

We awoke early the next morning in the fort to the sound of thunder. To my relief, the second hand on my dad's dad's watch was ticking around at normal speed. Boo's watch indicated six thirty, the same as mine. After stowing the cigarettes and matches in our canvas tote bags and putting the bags in the back of the fort where they would stay relatively dry, we grabbed our sleeping bags and comic books and ran to the back porch on my house. We talked about last night's venture in hushed tones, still not believing it was all true.

My dad and I were the only early risers in my family, so my mom and sisters were still asleep. My dad was already on his way to work. I would have to wait until later to return the watch to its proper place. Forty-five years later, my dad gave me the watch, reminding me of that summer, Boo, Teak-qua, and Moonbeam.

The room next to the porch was my bedroom, so no one would have heard what we were discussing. My parent's bedroom was on the front of the house and my sisters slept in the attic near the front of the house. My sisters were, no doubt, sleeping and dreaming of Farley Granger. His pictures adorned the walls, the slanted ceiling of the attic, and the mirrors over their dressers. Farley Granger was a contract actor with MGM. He was farmed out to a lot of "B movies," two of which my sisters had seen recently. In *The Naked Street*, a mobster (Anthony Quinn) saves Granger from the electric chair. Quinn's sister was pregnant with Granger's baby. *The Girl in the Red Velvet Swing* was the story of Evelyn Nesbitt (Joan Collins), who is pursued by a playboy architect (Ray Milland) and a millionaire (Farley Granger).

On a previous day, Boo and I wandered into the attic and noticed the pictures of Farley everywhere. In our most mischievous mood, we took the pictures down and, like a dog marking its territory, we peed on each and every one of them. Not a lot of pee, just a drop or two on each one, but we nailed them all. In adulthood, when I told my sisters what we did, they told me, with disgusted looks on their faces, that they used to kiss Farley good night before going to sleep. So they were now asleep, dreaming of Farley, with a little pee on their lips.

We put our sleeping bags and comic books in a corner to keep dry. The lightning was distant and the thunder muffled. The storm was close enough to begin raining. As the large drops started to pelt the roof of the porch, we moved inside to spread peanut butter and jelly on graham crackers. We took them back out to the porch with metal cups filled with milk. We sat on the metal glider, ate, watched the rain, and drank our milk.

In those days, milk was actually delivered by truck from Oyster's Dairy, a local milk farm. The milkman put the paper-capped bottles on the back porch. Prior to the fifties, a horse-drawn wagon delivered raw milk cooled with big blocks of ice. On hot, summer days, we used to ask the driver for chunks of ice. He would bust off pieces with his ice pick and give them to us, which we would suck on until our mouths went numb. It must have been clean ice, since none of us got sick. I remember the delivered raw milk separating as it sat on the back porch, the cream rising to the top against the paper cap. My mom would scrape some of the cream off and put it in her coffee.

Today was not the delivery day, so we had the porch to ourselves. We discussed how we would spend the rainy day. I brought up the idea of making rocket fuel. Boo was interested.

"How?" he asked.

"I read about it in the book that came with my chemistry lab," I said.

I got a chemistry lab for Christmas. The lab came with a book for conducting experiments with the supplied chemicals. The first thing I tried to make was gunpowder with sulfur, carbon, and potassium nitrate. It did nothing but smoke.

I didn't tell Boo that I tried making rocket fuel once before. I used the stove in our kitchen. It was on a Saturday, one of the few my dad was not working. He was in the breakfast nook just off the kitchen, sitting, reading the paper with his back to me. My sisters were not home, and Mom was at the beauty parlor. I melted sugar in a test tube over the gas flame on the left front burner. When the sugar became runny, I removed the tube from the flame, and emptied the potassium nitrate crystals from the chemistry set supplies into the sugar syrup. I stirred the mixture with a glass rod. It wasn't mixing well, and the sugar was solidifying. What I did next was one of those lessons learned that stays with you the rest of your life.

I re-heated the test tube containing the mixture. The flames from the stove were enough to ignite the mixture. Whoosh! The fuel completely burned, filling the kitchen with a fog-like white smoke. Luckily, the flames and spewing fuel were directed against the metal, drip coffeemaker on the right front burner. My dad never looked up from the paper. All he said was—

"What are you doing?" To which I replied—

"Making rocket fuel."

"Well, clean it up before your mother gets home," he said.

I opened the kitchen window and the back door, clearing the smoke. I then wiped off the coffeepot, which, miraculously, suffered no damage. By the time my dad finished the paper, the smoke, and most of the smell, was gone. I quietly put my chemistry set away and left the house, thanking Jesus for letting me live another day.

"All we have to do," I continued, "is melt sugar and put in some saltpeter."

"What's saltpeter?" Boo asked.

"Potassium nitrate," I said. "We can get some at the drugstore."

This I knew from experience. My dad worked with a man who had a small farm in the country. One summer, for a week, I was "farmed out" to him to help with the chores. I would help them cut and bale hay, feed the animals, and other farm-like duties. His sons were still quite young, so I was a big help to him. After the chores were done, I enjoyed riding the mules and digging tunnels in the hay in the barn with his sons and daughters. One time he caught me kissing his oldest daughter in the loft, and that was the end of my work on the farm. Before the kiss, I went to the drugstore with him, and he bought saltpeter. He said he used it to cure certain ailments in the cattle. That was a good enough answer for me.

"Okay," Boo said, as he washed the last graham cracker down, emptying his cup of milk. "Let's get goin'."

I took in the empty cups and put them in the sink. Boo had left his yellow rain coat at my house from the previous day's carbide pellet exploits. We donned our rain gear and headed for Turner's Drugstore. After we bought the saltpeter, we went around to the back of the store. I searched around in the trash and found what I was looking for. The drugstore was also a film-developing outlet for 35-mm cameras. I pocketed the empty canisters, and we headed back to my house.

When we got back, we used a candle to melt the sugar in an empty shoe-polish lid. We found the lid in my garage, along with the pliers we used to hold it over the flame. Soon the sugar melted, and we removed it from the candle. My science book did not give proportions, so we mixed an equal amount of saltpeter into the gooey substance. The saltpeter seemed to blend with the sugar easily enough. This time I did not reintroduce the mixture to the flame. Just as we finished, I heard my mom inside making coffee.

My sisters were still asleep in the attic, which was finished into a large bedroom.

"What now?" Boo asked.

"We let it cool while we get the rockets ready," I told him.

We took the empty film canisters to the garage. They were metal canisters, not like the plastic ones today. The canisters were the perfect shape. The screw-on lids were nippled out. We punched a hole in the lids from the inside, using a hammer and a nail. When we screwed the lids back onto the cans, they resembled little rocket engines. I got the design idea from looking at rocket kits advertised in a comic book. We returned to the porch, but the rocket fuel was not quite cool enough. I put Boo to work fanning the fuel with his hands. There was one more item needed for our first rocket launch. I went into the house to search for it.

"What are you doing out on the porch?" my mom asked.

She was still taller than I, but not by much. Her hair was brushed out, shoulder length, brown, and wavy. While Boo's mom was wiry, mine was Italian, and although not fat, she was always battling her weight. She used to eat these little brown candies about the size of a sugar cube. They were called Ayds and were supposed to curb your appetite. She went through a lot of them while fasting during Lent. She had on a housecoat (they weren't called robes then) and slippers. She was busy pouring herself her first cup of coffee, so when I said, "Making rockets," she did not flinch.

"Well don't make a mess," was all she said. She turned her attention back to yesterday's crossword puzzle.

I rummaged around in the living room closet until I found the near-empty roll of wrapping paper. I carefully removed the remainder of the paper and took the three-foot cardboard roll.

"What is that for?" mom asked, as I made my way through the kitchen on my way back to the back porch.

"It's our rocket launcher," I explained, as I grabbed some Ohio Blue Tip matches from the dispenser near the gas stove.

"Oh, well don't set the house on fire," she said, and turned back to her coffee and crossword.

Boo was still waving his hands over the sugar-saltpeter mixture as I closed the back door behind me.

"Let's break it into pieces," I said. "It should be cooled off by now."

We set about breaking the fuel into pieces. It was the color and consistency of peanut brittle without the peanuts, and it broke into shards. When we had small enough pieces, we put them in the film canisters and put the punctured lids back on.

"What are we going to use for a fuse?" Boo asked.

"Some of these pieces are long and thin," I said. "We can stuff them in the holes and light them. They will burn inside and light the rest of the fuel." I did not have to tell Boo what the cardboard tube was for. He figured that out as soon as he saw them.

"Hold the tube while I light off the first one," I said. I handed him the tube.

Boo rested the tube against the concrete porch floor and aimed it toward the woods. I inserted our first rocket into the bottom and dragged the Blue Tip against the side of my pants like I saw the dirty man do on our first sojourn. The friction lit the kitchen match, and I applied it to the shard sticking out of the canister lid. What happened next was awe-inspiring.

The shard sputtered at first, but then caught fire. Boo looked down at the bottom of the tube and did not see our first rocket streak out the other end, but I did. I also noticed he had moved the tube so that it aimed directly toward a large maple tree between the porch and the woods. As I watched open-mouthed, a white rope of smoke, connected to the end of the tube, headed straight for the tree. I let out a little cuss word.

"Shit," I said.

"Bang," the rocket replied as it hit the tree and exploded. My sisters screamed from the safety of their beds in the attic, no doubt awake now.

My mom looked out the window from the breakfast nook. She waved her finger, reminding me that she told me not to set the house on fire. Boo looked up to see the rocket bouncing back from the tree in a ball of smoke and purple flame. It was a good thing we did not load the first one with more fuel than we did, because it burned itself out before it scorched the grass around the tree. The rain would not have helped extinguish the flame, because this was rocket fuel, and it could burn under water.

"Damn, Boo," I said. "Hold the tube straight." In the excitement of launching our first rocket, I forgot to make the sign of the cross for my two swear words.

"I will," he said. "But did you see that? It would have gone to Cherry Avenue if it hadn't hit the tree."

Our next launch went better, but did not make it over the Watson Woods and onto Cherry Avenue. We used up all but three pieces of the rocket fuel on the next two launches. We decided making rockets was okay, but something we could do later. I put the pieces of fuel in my pocket. The rest of the morning was spent reading comic books until the rains stopped. When the sun came out, the humidity dropped and the world started to dry up. Boo and I split up and went our separate ways until nightfall.

Again, that night we tried to stay awake to see if Teak-qua appeared, but we only drifted off into sleep. I awoke to Boo shaking me vigorously.

"Wake up, wake up," he said. "Teak-qua's here."

"Where?" I asked, in a groggy state, rubbing my eyes. I sat up and looked to the rear of the fort to see the by-now familiar face of Teak-qua smoking his pipe.

"How was your trip last night, my little warriors?" Teak-qua asked.

"It went okay," Boo said. He was more alert at the moment than I was. "We wasted the bad guys. It was cool, watching the colonel fall on his own severed arm. Who was that guy and where were we?" Boo was not smoking, so I did not light one up either.

"You were not far from here," Teak-qua said. "He was a man who was partly responsible for my death. His name was Colonel David Williamston. The people he killed were of the Moravian tribe, allies of my people, the Delaware tribe." Pointing to me with the stem of his pipe, he continued. "They were the people I told you about the first night we met. They have been avenged, and can now sleep in peace. The time was seventeen hundred and eighty-one."

"More who-vians?" Boo asked, not understanding.

"I'll tell you later," I said.

"Where are we going tonight?" I asked, regaining some of my consciousness. "It would help if we knew where we are and who we are looking for. What if we get the wrong person?"

"You will always see the atrocity and the one who caused it," Teak-qua responded. "If you really want to know, I will tell you the story before you go on your ride."

"Why can't we get them before they kill the Indians?" Boo asked.

I looked at Boo, jealous that I had not posed the question first.

"Because then they would not have done anything wrong," was Teak-qua's response.

I looked back at Teak-qua with a smile. Now I was glad I had not asked the question.

"My people will rest in peace just knowing they have been avenged," Teak-qua continued. "They have died once. It is not necessary to save them first and have them die in a different way, at another time and place."

"Suppose we are not successful?" I asked. "We were lucky we had dynamite last night, and a way to blow it up."

"You are resourceful warriors," Teak-qua said. "You will always find cleverness when the time comes. Tonight you will travel not as far back in time, less than one hundred years, but you will be further away. Moonbeam will take you to where the Beaver Creek and Bear River meet in a place you call Idaho. You will join our people there for what will seem a long time. When Moonbeam brings you home it will only have been for the night. You will awake tomorrow morning refreshed as if you slept the night away. The memory will remain with you, but not the passing of time. This time do not forget your rifles."

Boo and I looked at each other, embarrassed we left our guns behind last night after he told us to always take them.

"That reminds me," Boo said, tilting his head to one side. "Our watches don't work when we go back."

"They work," I corrected. "But they go real slow."

"You have no need for telling the time," Teak-qua assured us. "You will always get back before morning."

Boo and I both snickered and almost said what we both were thinking. *Watches, watches, we don't need no stinking watches.*

"What else will we need?" I asked, trying to hold back a smile.

"You will have all you need," Teak-qua responded, but Boo took his Roy Rogers watch anyway. I had put my dad's dad's watch back in his dresser the previous afternoon.

We found Moonbeam in the field as we did the night before. We were again glad that wading out to the island was not necessary. When we crossed the barbed-wire fence, I found a discarded ball of hay-baling twine, which I recognized from work on the farm. I picked it up, and tossed it into the canvas bag.

Moonbeam was glad to see us. We both had apples, picked from David's backyard tree, to give her. She ate the apples and gave us each a nose bump in return. I got on her back first using a boost from Boo. I then hoisted Boo up behind me. The third trip made us experts at getting onto Moonbeam in this manner. We sat straight in the saddle and let Moonbeam take us on a ride, first over the city so we could make out landmarks below.

"Look," I said, pointing to the right. "There is State Street School." State Street School was the junior high school I would attend at the beginning of the school year. It is no longer there.

"Yeah," Boo said, pointing further to the south. "There's Mike's Warehouse." Mike's Warehouse was a little grocery store we passed on our way to grade school. We never stole from Mike's. We bought candy there when we had a nickel. Mike sometimes had sample dog biscuits sitting out so we could take some to the dogs we encountered on the way to and from school. I used to eat some of the biscuits just to see what they tasted like. They had a piquant flavor and an aftertaste that could only be erased with peanut butter.

At the end of the journey, the ribbons of light returned to the twinkle of stars. The moon was waxing in the west. The sun was chasing the darkness of night with a crest of deep to light blue in the east. Moonbeam circled over a barren landscape. A light dusting of snow provided a sharp contrast to a dark, narrow river, which wound itself through the gently rolling and, except for along the river, treeless land. From the place Moonbeam was circling, the river snaked south and slightly east, and then north and east. As we circled ever lower, the moon, low on the horizon, began to bounce light off the river as it crisscrossed beneath us to the west. Nearing the ground, we noticed a smaller creek flowing into the larger river.

"This must be where the Bear River and Beaver Creek meet," I said, remembering what Teak-qua told us.

"Look, off to the left, there are teepees," Boo said. Right then, unlike the last trip, I started to feel the cold.

"We're going to freeze our asses off," Boo said, starting to feel the cold too. The metamorphosis had transpired, making us into late teenagers, but the clothes we wore were still jeans and T-shirts. As soon as Moonbeam stopped on firm soil, we both hopped off. I grabbed the transformed saddlebags and looked inside.

"Damn," I said. "There ain't no clothes inside. We **are** going to freeze our asses off."

"We can cut the hide off Moonbeam if we have to," Boo said. This elicited a look toward us from Moonbeam that was one of horror and disgust.

"Don't even kid about that," I said in Moonbeam's defense. "I wouldn't let you do that, and how would we get back, dipshit?" Dipshit is something I heard the older boys call each other, and I had no idea what it meant. I was so cold I could not even make the sign of the cross for the minor swear-word infraction.

Shivering, Boo said, "Let's go and see if the Indians will give us something warm." As if to tell us that was a good idea, Moonbeam nudged me in the back with her nose, urging me to move toward the village.

We held our rifles close to our chest as we hugged ourselves trying to keep in as much warmth as we could. We were within

73

three hundred feet of the camp, when the sun started to come up in the southeast. There was nothing to impede the progress of the rising sun, and by the time we reached the edge of the village, the top of the teepees were bathed in a warm, orange glow. Smoke was wafting out from the top of the tent-like homes, reaching straight up to embrace the morning rays. There was activity in what seemed to be the center of the village. Horses near the water were making their snorting noises as they too welcomed the anticipated morning warmth of the sun.

When we got close, two dogs charged toward us, barking a warning to the inhabitants of the closest teepee. Almost at once, an Indian wearing a buffalo skin came out to see what all the fuss was about. Boo and I both stopped, and I thought, *Uh-oh! We may be in trouble now. What if they think were attacking?* Moonbeam stopped alongside of us and whinnied, at the same time pawing at the ground. As if in understanding, the Indian turned and shouted to the village—

"They're here." Only it sounded funny. It was as if he spoke a different language, but I understood every word.

"Did you understand that?" I asked Boo.

"Yeah," he said. "At first it sounded strange, but then I got exactly what he said."

"Well, let's keep going," I said. "I'm colder than a well digger's ass in Montana." I learned this saying from my father, and ass, although a swear word, was a lesser sin, not worthy of a sign of the cross.

The buffalo skin–wearing Indian was walking out to meet us with his arms spread wide, as if we were long lost relatives. He was tall and walked with a deep gait. It was almost as if he were stretching his legs out with each step. His naked head was adorned with long, jet-black hair tied from the forehead back with rawhide. The end of his hair hung midway down his back. He had a chiseled, handsome face that was at the same time rugged looking. He wore animal skin boots, laced up the side with rawhide. Dressed as he was in animal fur, it was as if a large bear was about to envelop us both. In fact, he did grab us both at the same time, just as we let our rifles drop to our sides. It was a strong and firm hug, crushing us together like grapes in a winepress.

"I am One-Who-Touches-Bear," he said, again sounding strange, but I understood every word. "Welcome to our village. The Shoshone people have been expecting you. Teak-qua told us you would be in need of clothing, so we have skins for both of you."

"Where is Teak-qua?" Boo asked.

I turned and looked at Boo as he spoke, not believing my ears. His words came out in a foreign language, but, just like Touches-Bear, I understood what he said. It took a few seconds for me to realize that, along with our physical transformation, we also picked up a linguistic skill. Boo also was startled by what he said.

"We're speaking their language," I said to Boo, this time in English. "Not only that, we can understand it."

"Yeah, no shit," Boo said in English. "Did they say they were Shoshone?" The Indian looked confused, not understanding what we were saying.

"I'm sorry," I said, directing my words toward the Indian. I too was able to speak his language. "Where is Teak-qua?"

"Yes," I said to Boo, in English. "He did say Shoshone." It seemed we could change back and forth from English to Shoshone at will.

"Teak-qua appears in the smoke from the fire and speaks to us," Touches-Bear explained. "He told us you would come and avenge our people."

"But Teak-qua said you would be dead," Boo said. "We only come in after the damage has been done."

"Teak-qua is a wise and great medicine man," Touches-Bear said. "If that is what he says, then it is true." He turned to look over his shoulder as a girl came out of the teepee carrying two fur coats. Boo and I both looked around Touches-Bear, me to his left and Boo to his right. What we saw made both of us raise our eyebrows and tilt our heads back in disbelief.

"It's Bobbie-Lou," I said, in English. Bobbie-Lou was a girl my age, who lived across from Boo on Watson Avenue. When all of the Watson Avenue gang played kickball on those warm, summer nights, Bobbie-Lou wore tight-fitting shorts. We used to kid her by chanting, *Bobbie-Lou with the shorts up her cu.* Cu was the Italian word for butt; therefore, like caca, cu was not a swear word. It was probably how the word for the women's dress, culottes, was derived. We kidded her but liked to look at her butt just the same.

"It can't be," Boo responded. "But it sure looks like her, all growed up." I didn't correct his English this time. "I wonder if Mugsy is here too."

Mugsy was Bobbie-Lou's little pug dog. Mugsy always had a cinder rock in his mouth and ran all over the neighborhood, looking for someone to play fetch. He used to fetch that cinder rock so often, it would be spotted with blood from his gums. We used to like to toss the rock into places he could not go, but he was always able to retrieve his favorite toy. Once Boo tossed the rock into a neighbor's bushes. We heard a crash as the rock went through the basement window. We would have run away, but poor Mugsy was trying to get in through the busted glass to get his rock. We had to knock on the door and tell them what had happened, and beg, "Please give us Mugsy's rock back." We left out, "… before he kills himself jumping through the window."

Mugsy met his demise shortly thereafter at the hands of a student driver. He was retrieving his rock that was just tossed across the street. After hitting Mugsy, the driver did not stop. David and his brother chased the car down with their bikes. They caught the driver and the instructor two streets over. When the car stopped, they asked the instructor why he didn't stop. He just shrugged it off and kept on going. Bobbie-Lou witnessed the "accident," but there was nothing that could be done for poor old Mugsy. We really missed that dog. We buried his rock with him.

The young girl, not at all embarrassed by the strangers and our different language, strode out to us, proffering the coats. As she handed one to me, our hands brushed and a tingle went up my arm. She smiled, and I thought, *Perhaps she felt it too*. Touches-Bear looked from her to me and smiled. *Damn, is it that obvious?* I said to myself. She looked identical to Bobbie-Lou, only a taller version. She had Bobbie-Lou's dark, smiling eyes. Unlike Touches-Bear, her black hair was not tied back, but cascaded gently like a waterfall out from under her beaded headband, splashing out onto her shoulders. Her nose was straight, long, and had a slight bump in the middle, and accented her full lips. Her olive oil–colored face was heart-shaped with high cheekbones. She wore a buckskin dress tied at her narrow waist, culminating over high, laced, moccasin boots. As she turned to go back to the teepee, I noticed the fullness of her breasts and the soft curves of her buttocks. *There's Bobbie-Lou with the shorts up her cu.*

"That is my sister, Nightstar," Touches-Bear said, anticipating what was on my mind.

"Damn, she's good-lookin'," Boo said, thankfully in English.

"She's very pretty," I managed to blurt out. I wanted to ask if she had a boyfriend, but did not. It would have been interesting to see how "boyfriend" translated. I was feeling urges I did not understand, most likely a result of the temporary transformation from boy to teenager.

"You are in time for breakfast," Touches-Bear said. "We are cooking rabbit, and have some flatbread baking near the fire. After you eat, we will meet Chief Bear Hunter and some of the other warriors. Then we will go hunting."

Boo and I said nothing more as we tried on our new "skins." They fit fine, albeit a bit heavy. They were warm and comfortable, but smelled like the horses at the White Horse riding stable. We followed Touches-Bear to a fire pit near the center of the village. Moonbeam parted from us and walked toward the water, where the other horses were grazing.

Warriors surrounded the fire pit, sitting cross-legged with painted faces. Bits of meat were on long skewers roasting over the hot outer coals of a ten-foot diameter ring of rocks. The radiating heat from the coals warmed our bodies. As we approached, an older woman offered a canteen filled with water. The metal canteen was covered with tan wool, and had a cork in the mouth tethered to the side with a metal chain. She held it out to us by the long, white, cloth sling that went around the container. From a family trip to Gettysburg three summers ago, I recognized it as being from the Civil War. Moonbeam must have taken us back to the 1860s. I took the canteen, but was not thirsty, or hungry, for that matter. I remembered our last trip when we neither drank nor ate. Lack of thirst and appetite would make sense if we were gone for only one night. If we are here for what seems a longer period, I wondered if the same would hold true. I took a drink so that I would not offend our hosts and passed the canteen to Boo. Boo took a similar, ceremonial sip. We then sat down, crossing our legs Indian style.

One of the men stood and offered us a skewer with a chunk of meat the size of a hot dog. Smoke drifted off the meat along its length. I laid my rifle on the ground as I reached for the meat and thanked him in his own language. I blew on the meat and tore off a chunk with my fingers. The warrior smiled as he took another skewer and ate the meat directly. I chewed the meat, which was tough yet tasty. I then passed the skewer to Boo after he laid his rifle down next to mine.

"Thank you," I said to him and then to the woman.

"You're welcome," they replied simultaneously.

The older woman then offered flatbread to both of us. Boo held his flatbread in one open hand and then wiped his bit of meat from the skewer as if he were putting it in a hot dog in a bun. The Indians watched him quizzically, and then, as if they thought it was a good idea, they did the same. Too bad there wasn't any ketchup to put on it. We would have really showed them something. I took a bite out of the flatbread, chewed, and swallowed as best I could, lacking something to wash it down with.

As we finished our breakfast, Nightstar came to the fire pit. There were several other young girls with her, but she was the most attractive. The others were looking at Boo and me and giggled as only young girls can. Nightstar glanced up once in my direction and smiled. The other girls looked at her when she did this, and I thought I saw a blush come to her cheeks. I was entranced, but the spell was soon broken by Touches-Bear.

"You will meet Chief Hunts Bear now," Touches-Bear said. We stood up when Touches-Bear did and followed him toward one of the larger teepees.

Touches-Bear held open the flap to the teepee and gestured for us to enter. When we got inside, heat radiated from the fire in the middle of the tent. On the far side sat an older man. On either side of him were two larger braves. They were as big as football players, except they were not fat. The old man was wrapped in a blanket. His hair was tied back like Teak-qua's, and he wore the same type of pants and boots. We could not tell if he was wearing anything other than the blanket around his back.

"Welcome to our camp," Hunts Bear said. "We understand you were sent by Teak-qua to avenge some of the wrongs to our people. You are welcome here as if you were my own sons." He gestured toward the two braves sitting on either side of him, obviously his real sons. "We would like to take you on a hunt with us today. Then tonight, we will feast, if we are successful hunters. Teak-qua tells me you are both good with your guns. We can always use two more good hunters." The brave on his right, who looked to be the younger of the two, gave a dissatisfied grunt. We sensed he was not pleased with our presence among the Indians. One look from his father kept him from grunting anymore.

"As you can tell, there is some uneasiness with your presence," he continued. White men came to our valley three years ago. They are taking over all the land to farm. They also are taking over all the rivers, so that it is getting hard for us to survive. That is why we must go long distances to hunt. I cannot go with you today, for I am getting too old to hunt, and the cold bothers me more than it used to. But I will welcome you back tonight. I bid you good hunting."

"Thank you," Boo said.

"Yes, I thank you too," I said, although it sounded silly. Touches-Bear put one hand on each of our shoulders and tugged us toward the entrance to the teepee. The two sons eyed us with suspicion, making me feel uncomfortable.

"I don't think his sons want us around," I said, once we were outside the teepee.

"They are hot-headed warriors," Touches-Bear said. "Hunts Bear has had trouble lately with them pulling raids on the settlers. So far they have only been sneaking into the settlers' farms at night and stealing animals and food, but I fear they would do more if their father let them.

"Let us go hunt," he said, slapping us on our backs. "There are bear and antelope nearby. We will ride toward the mountains in the west." We followed him to where a group of men were on horseback. The chief's sons were right behind us. Moonbeam was waiting amidst the other hunters.

"Did you say bear?" I asked.

"Yes," Touches-Bear said. "They make good blankets, and the meat is good. We will find out how brave you are."

"I thought bear hibernated in the winter?" I asked.

"They do," answered Touches-Bear. "This is not winter, it is late fall. The bears are getting the last bit of food to fatten up for their long winter's sleep. They are not as cautious as in the summer."

I said nothing else as we headed toward the horses. The stirring in my groin I felt previously, when Nightstar and the other girls came into view, changed to a stirring in my stomach. I had only been hunting once with my uncle and that was for rabbits. This would be a little different than shooting birds in the Watson Woods, or rabbits in a field with a hunting dog.

Five

Riding double, which brought a look of disapproval from the other Indians, but not from Touches-Bear, Boo and I followed the trek westward, resting our rifles in front of us on Moonbeam's back. Unlike the sparse vegetation we were riding through, pine trees painted the top half of the three-thousand-foot mountains ahead a pale green. Without saying a word, the Indians urged their horses into a gallop. As Moonbeam increased her gait to keep up, the earlier looks of disapproval turned into jealous stares. Moonbeam's movements were smooth as silk, allowing Boo and me to sit up straight, holding only our rifles. The others were clutching their horses' manes. One tried to imitate us and let go. When he did this, he almost fell off his horse; the terrain was so rough. Touches-Bear smiled, knowing that Moonbeam was special. Even as we began the gradual ascent to the trees through large outcroppings of rock, Boo and I were still able to keep our balance, taking in the scenery around us.

As if someone gave a signal, everyone stopped and dismounted, allowing the horses to rest and graze on the sparse vegetation just below the tree line. Boo checked in with Roy on his wristwatch.

"It's just one fifteen," he said in English. "We must have a couple of days to go, what with all the faster time is moving."

Touches-Bear gave a disapproving glance in our direction and held one finger to his lips. He then pointed in the direction of the trees. We followed, bending low as the others were doing, holding our rifles out for balance. In about thirty paces we were in the woods, looking for what, Boo and I had no idea. The Indians were spreading themselves out, about fifty feet between each of them. Boo and I did the same, only we kept within twenty-five feet of each other. It seemed like we crept close to the ground for a half mile or more. My thighs were beginning to burn. I could tell Boo was feeling the same because he kept rubbing the tops of his legs.

Again, without saying a word, the rest of the hunting party dropped to the ground and began to crawl very slowly. We took our cue from them and did the same. I had no idea what was in store, other than that we were going after some unknown game, unknown to Boo and me, that is. Then I remembered. *Bear,* I thought to myself. *We're after bears. We're gonna get killed.* When our hunting companions stopped, we stopped. When they started their alligator-like crawl again, we crawled.

Then everyone took a position behind a pine tree. We followed suit, as if we were waiting to ambush someone or thing. It wasn't long before my fears were rewarded, for crawling on all fours almost straight for us were two brown bears. It was a mother and her cub. I had never seen a real live grizzly bear before, but read that they can weigh eight hundred pounds. This one was a female, and a little smaller. The cub was almost full grown, probably in its second year with the mother. My guess was she was about four hundred, and the cub about the same size. I could hear no noise from anything but the foraging bear and her cub. There was a slight breeze coming down the side of the mountain. Had the wind been blowing toward the bear, they would have picked up our scent long before we saw them, and we would never have known they were there.

The cub was some distance behind the mother. Our cover was so good, the mother walked between Boo and me on her right, and two others from our hunting party on her left. She went about twenty yards behind us when it happened.

As quiet as we tried to be, one of the two Indians on the other side of the mother bear turned to watch her. It was Chief Hunts Bear's youngest son. As he did so, he reached out to grab one of the low-hanging branches from the pine tree he was behind. It snapped and he fell forward. The mother bear was quick. She turned and saw the source of the noise, saw that her cub was separated from her, and instinctively charged the sprawling Indian. The cub raised up to see what was going on around him, spotted one of the other Indians, who stood up to get a better shot at the charging mother, and commenced a charge of his own.

Having my rifle already pointed in the general direction of the mother, I quickly aimed and shot. Boo drew a bead on the cub and just as quickly fired at him. I watched as my shot went straight into the left side of the mother, just below her left ear. By then she was nearly on top of the hapless hunter. She fell dead, as the right side of her head exploded outward, and landed with a thud on top of the prone Indian, pinning him underneath.

Boo's shot also found its mark and, like mine, took off the side of the cub's head opposite the entry wound. There was no need for either of us to shoot again. As the smoke from our rifles wisped away in the slight breeze, the rest of the hunting party emerged and headed toward the fallen prey.

Immediately, two of the Indians fell upon the fallen bears with knives. They turned the bears over and cut deep into their chests. As Boo and I cautiously approached, still wary of the size of the animals, the rest of the hunting party came close to us and grabbed us by the shoulders and rubbed our hair.

"You are first-caliber hunters," Touches-Bear said, smiling. "You also may have saved the lives of one of our braves and the chief's youngest son. We can use braves with your shooting skills to help fight against the white man."

"We just aimed and shot," I said in my best "aw-shucks" impersonation.

"Still, you were very quick and accurate," Touches-Bear responded. "My best braves could not have dropped the bears with only one shot each. You must have some magic. That is why they were touching your hair, in hopes of some of it rubbing off on them. Now, come and taste the spoils of the hunt."

"Taste the spoils?" I said to Boo.

"I hope that doesn't mean what I think it does," Boo said, in English with an upturned corner of his left lip. It meant worse than he and I thought.

As we followed Touches-Bear back toward the knife-brandishing hunting companions, they were reaching into the bloody chest of both of the bears. Wide eyed, we watched as they pulled first the heart of the mother and then the cub out of their respective chests. They were dripping in blood and, I swear, still beating. They may have just been quivering, but I couldn't believe what happened next. The hearts were lifted in outstretched hands to Boo and me.

"It is your honor to take the first bite," Touches-Bear said.

"Screw you!" Boo said, thankfully in English.

My reaction was not that strong, but the look on my face must have startled the rest of the hunting party.

"You must," Touches-Bear said. "This is a great honor. It would be an insult to refuse." He was smiling when he said this. I half suspected it was a ruse, but I could not be sure.

"Hell," I said, making a mental note of the venial sin for my next confession. "I've eaten turnips and even caster oil; I guess I can gag down a bleeding, beating, warm, bear heart." Thankfully this also came out in English.

"You go first," Boo said, looking at me like I was the biggest fool he ever saw.

This was not the first time I had seen a beating heart yanked from the chest of an animal. My dad was a meat inspector for the state of Ohio when I was six or seven years old. One day he took me on one of his inspections to a local slaughterhouse. I don't know what his intentions were, but I went along. The sweet, sickening smell as we entered the main slaughtering area, remains with me and always will. We passed a lot of animal carcasses hanging from hooks and moving slowly along an assembly line (or should it have been called a disassembly line?). Anyway, we got to the back part of the building where live cows and steers were being herded into pens. It was dark and smelled of piss and shit. The cow I witnessed was led from the back lot into a narrow, inside pen that had steel bars lining the sides and front. It was a black and white cow, which I later found out was a Holstein. It also could have been a bull, but as a kid everything was a cow. This one, obviously, was not raised to produce milk, or was past its prime.

The cow must have smelled fear or felt impending doom. As it was led into the narrow stall, it tried to back out, only there was a man in a red-splotched, white apron behind it, slamming a black, steel gate shut. The cow's eyes got huge as a large bar was place down around its neck, pinning it in place. I was standing only three feet from it, where its mooing was quite deafening. As I watched in utter (no pun intended) amazement, the man who had closed the gate walked around to face the cow. My dad was holding a clipboard in one hand and a pencil in the other. The man reached over on a table and grabbed a pistol. In one swift movement, he pointed the pistol at the center of the cow's head between its giant, wide eyes. I heard the loud crack of the gun, which echoed in the small room. I then knew the red splotches on the man's apron were cow blood splattered from the cow's head at the moment the bullet entered.

Immediately, the cow dropped as far as it could in the pen. Its bladder let loose, and piss came pouring out of it and onto the floor. My dad made a note on the clipboard. The man then went around behind the lifeless animal and stuck a hook in either leg. A chain was lowered from the ceiling and connected to the hooks. The cow was then hoisted up and back through the now-open gate. It was shoved along the disassembly line to an area with a large curb around it. The man then took a hose and washed the animal with some sort of greenish solution. My dad made some more annotations on the clipboard.

Placing a hand on my shoulder, he guided me to the other side of the hanging carcass, to where another man in a bloodier apron was wielding a knife. He proceeded to cut the cow from top to bottom, allowing guts and, to me, unidentifiable things fall out onto the floor. Needless to say, there was a lot of blood mixed in when the cow was turned inside out. The man reached into the open area created with the knife and proceeded to pull out organs as he cut them free.

My eyes became glued to one item in particular. It was the cow's heart, still beating when the second man placed it on the table behind him. My dad made some more notes, and then put his hand on my back guiding me out of the room and into the colder areas where the cows were being cut quite quickly into pieces. As we walked past the table, my eyes remained on the beating heart, my head swiveling as the rest of me, from the neck down, followed my dad from the killing room. My memory of that day was recalled the moment I saw the beating heart.

My mind released the thought of the butcher shop's beating heart as I walked up to the Indian who was straddling the bear I shot.

His hands were still holding the pulsing heart toward me, slightly shaking up and down, as if motioning me to come on and eat before it got cold. I looked at the faces of those around me, and they were not smiling but looked as if they were at High Mass in the middle of a sermon.

I held out an open hand, in which he immediately dumped the heart. It was more than warm, it was almost hot, and yes, it was pulsing, beating, and dripping in blood. I slowly lifted it toward my mouth, my lips quivering as if my dad had just given me an ass whipping. Thankfully, there was no bad smell, but I held my breath just the same. Blood ran down my forearm and dripped off my elbow. I opened my mouth, keeping my tongue far back in my throat. As my lips touched the heart, I opened my mouth about as wide as I could stand. Wanting to get this over with, I put the heart past my teeth and took a bite. I tore off a piece by yanking my hand away. Fighting a gag, I made an attempt to chew, but swallowed the piece nearly whole.

Blood was running down my chin as I handed the heart back to the smiling Indian. He then took a hearty bite and passed the rendered heart to the brave next to him. Touches-Bear was smiling as if I were his son.

All eyes turned to Boo, who was standing there with his mouth open so far, his chin almost touched his chest.

"Your turn," I said, with a grin exposing bloody teeth and lips.

"Okay, asshole," Boo said. He turned toward the Indian straddling the cub, reached out, and was presented with his trophy. I must admit he did better than I, and took a bigger chunk of the heart. He did gag once, but was able to swallow his piece just as I did. He then looked at me with the same gory smile. We simultaneously transferred the blood from our faces to our shirtsleeves.

"You now are as brave as the bear," Touches-Bear said. "All of us have the bear's courage, and since we shared the heart, some of your skills have passed to us. Let us take the spoils back to the village. None of the bear will be wasted, as you shall see. But first we must give thanks to the bears for giving their lives and souls to us."

We followed the lead of the others, kneeling on one knee, facing the bears, and bending our heads toward the earth. Touches-Bear chanted, and all were moving their lips, so Boo and I made up prayers of our own. I don't know what he said, but I thanked God for not letting the bear get to me first. I later asked Boo what he prayed for, but he refused to tell me.

"It's sacred," was his only response.

Small trees were cut, and sleds were made to which the bears were strapped. This was done while others retrieved the horses. Boo and I were glad to see Moonbeam approaching. We both smiled. I felt the remaining crusted blood on my face crack and fall off. We let the Indians tend to the bears while Boo and I got on Moonbeam and let her walk slowly around the whole scene. There was no more talking as we rode back to the camp, dragging the hapless bears. Boo looked at Roy Rogers and held it up for me to see. It was nearly two o'clock our time.

When we got back to the camp, the women took over while the men gathered around the center of the camp. We followed, leaving Moonbeam to her own devices. It looked like preparation was underway for a celebration. Fires were stoked and spears were readied for skewering the bear meat. We watched as Nightstar and the others skinned the bears and cut up the meat. Some of it they prepared in strips, which were hung on racks to dry. The fat was cut away and put in pots for rendering. The skins were to be scraped to remove the fat and membrane, and then rubbed with wood ash. The hides would be hung on racks to dry in the sun. Touches-Bear was right about not wasting any of the kill. Large pieces of bear meat were put on sticks and laid near the fire to cook. Bread was also laid on hot rocks taken from the fire to bake. After an hour of preparation, the meal began.

It was quite good, and Boo and I were surprised we were hungry. When we looked for something to drink, leather bags were passed around. We later found out they were buffalo balls filled with mead, or fermented honey. Pipes were passed around too. The Marlboros Boo and I pulled from our pockets got the immediate attention of the Indians. We lit ours in the fire and passed the others out to the braves. I looked around, but did not see any of the women. When we all were a little looped, the chief came over and sat next to us.

"I want to thank you for possibly saving the life of my son and one of the other braves," Hunts Bear said.

Possibly, I thought. *Those guys would have been dead meat if Boo and I weren't there. Maybe something was lost in the translation from Shoshone to English.*

"Because of your bravery," he continued, "I would like each of you to have these." He handed each of us a turquoise stone pendant hanging from a line of rawhide. He placed them over our heads and around our necks. As he did so, the others around the campfire started to hoot and whoop. I held mine out in front so I could see it better. The mottled blue of the stone reflected the dancing orange flames of the fire.

"Thank you, very much," I said. There were tears starting to form in my eyes, not so much from the gift, but from the smoke of the campfire.

"I thank you too," Boo said. "You know we will have to take these off when we get back, otherwise we'll be considered faggots." This last sentence was in English.

"I know what I want to do with mine someday," I replied, also in English.

During the eating and celebrating, darkness had overtaken us, and one by one the men were retiring to their teepees.

We looked around, wondering where we were supposed to go. Boo looked at his watch and declared it was only two fifteen, wondering if it was time to go back. We knew Moonbeam would come and get us if it were. I was exhausted and I could tell Boo was too. Touches-Bear's led us to his tent, which, once inside, was quite roomy. There was a small fire pit in the center and bearskins laid around the perimeter. Touches-Bear pointed to two skins on either side of the opening. Behind the fire I could make out the silhouettes of two other people. I assumed one was Touches-Bear's wife, and the other one could be Nightstar, but I wasn't sure. We laid our rifles down on the teepee side of the bearskins. It was obvious that we would sleep with our coats pulled over us.

"I sure hope they keep that fire goin', or it's going to be a cold night," I whispered to Boo, in English.

"I don't know," Boo said. "These skins are pretty warm. Warmer than the blankets I have on my bed at home. I sure hope Teak-qua is right about us not being gone more than a night, or my ass is grass and my mom's the lawnmower." He held Roy up to me to show me it was almost three our time.

"Teak-qua was right about us getting back before dawn the other two times, and we were in the other time zone the second time for an entire day," I reassured him, barely convincing myself.

"You two talk as much as old women," Teak-qua said. "At least you could speak our language so I could understand. Now, get to sleep. Tomorrow will come soon enough."

As I was about to fall asleep, there was a grunting and giggling sound coming from Touches-Bear and his wife. I didn't know what they were doing exactly, but they must have been making out. As their efforts were winding down, I heard a rustling as if someone were moving about the tent. I jumped when a body slid in beside me under the bearskin blanket. I started to open my mouth, but a gentle, sweet-smelling hand was placed over it.

"Be quiet," Nightstar whispered in my ear. She snuggled closer to me and started to undress. I panicked, but did not move away from her. "We can share the warmth better if you take off your clothes."

As I shed the last remnants of my clothes, she moved close to me. I was on my back. She was on her side next to me. Her long gossamer-like hair draped across my face. It was soft and sweet-smelling, as if she had rubbed flowers through it. Her chin was on my shoulder, and her warm breath was condensing on my neck. I felt lightning bolts of electricity shoot the length of my spine as she placed an arm across my chest and a leg across mine. She was warm, almost hot. I never felt such comfort.

She pulled her head away from mine, and I looked in her direction. Our lips met ever so gently and softly. It was only my second kiss, and I thought I could die on the spot and never miss anything again. The taste of her was more than sweet. It was metallic, warm, and satisfying.

"Go to sleep, my brave," she said. I was more tired than excited, so I obeyed.

When I awoke, Nightstar was not in my arms anymore. Sometime in the night, she must have awakened and returned to her bed. Sitting up, I could see Nightstar was in her bed, but Touches-Bear's bed was empty. Light was coming in from the half-opened flap of the tent. I was suddenly aware of the presence of another. I looked toward the entrance, and Moonbeam's large head was poking in the side of the flap. She snorted and shook her head up and down.

"Boo," I said, in a raspy voice. "Boo. Get up. Moonbeam wants something." Boo started to stir, as I pulled the bearskin back.

I immediately realized I was naked. I grabbed for my clothes, which were in a heap at the bottom of the skins. At first I was confused, and then I realized that maybe that was not a dream I had after all. Moonbeam was impatiently pawing at the ground.

"Boo, get up!" I shouted, suddenly finding my voice.

"Okay, okay," responded a groggy Boo. He started to pat the ground around his bed in a futile attempt to get at a cigarette.

"What time is it?" I asked. "Maybe we have to get back. Moonbeam seems very impatient."

"Three o'clock," Boo said squinting at Roy while rubbing the sleep out of his eyes with his other hand. "We can't go back. We haven't killed any bad guys."

"We didn't kill any bad guys the first time either," I said, pulling on my socks and reaching for my shoes. "Is it time to go, Moonbeam?" I asked, not expecting an answer. As if I could now speak in her language, just like I was understood by the Shoshone, she nodded her head up and down. I took that for a yes.

"I see it is time for you to go, my warriors," Touches-Bear exclaimed as he entered the tent next to Moonbeam. Moonbeam backed out, satisfied that we got the message. "You will be back in a couple of months. We will see you then. I will tell the others you said good-bye. They will understand."

"We'll be back?" I said. "How do you know that?"

"Teak-qua and I talk every night," he responded. "The next time, you will avenge my people. The others do not know what is to take place. It is only known to Teak-qua and myself." He walked toward me as I stood up, and we hugged each other. He held me

96

at arm's length with outstretched arms and looked directly into my eyes. "I would be proud to call you my son." He then walked over to Boo, who was also standing, and hugged him, only not as affectionately. I wondered if he knew that Nightstar and I shared the same bed last night. It still seemed like a dream. The best dream I ever had in my life. I reached in my pocket and took out the pendant I was given when we killed the bears. I tiptoed to where Nightstar was sleeping. I reached down and put the bauble around her neck. I left the rawhide strap untied so as not to wake her. She stirred a little, reached up, and touched the stone. She smiled but never opened her eyes. She slid the turquoise down her chest and moved it over her heart. I backed away as quietly as I had approached.

The three of us stepped out into the cool, autumn air. Moonbeam was anxiously waiting. Three minutes later, we were on Moonbeam, galloping across the plains. Then it was the same meteoric ride through the stars on our way back to the present.

Six

On our walk back from the park, I told Boo about my sharing the bed with Nightstar. I said I thought she was in bed with me and we kissed. Either that or it was a succubus. He asked me what that was. I told him I read about it in a book, and that it was a female demon that was supposed to have sex with a man when he slept. To us sex involved kissing and something else. He agreed that it must have been a dream. That was the end of our discussion about my dream.

As we walked passed the park entrance, a man's voice called out to us.

"What are you kids doing out this early in the morning?" came the booming voice of the dreaded Mr. Kidwell. He was standing beside the eight-foot-high stone tower that marked the north sidewalk park entrance from Union Avenue. He was in his typical dark clothing and was difficult to discern in the dim streetlight. "Don't you know there is a ten o'clock curfew for children under sixteen?" We were not "in the park," so we weren't in violation of his ban for killing the duck. It was good neither of us were smoking at the time.

"I was showing him my paper route, so he can do it for the next week," Boo responded. My heart had still not resumed beating when he blurted out the lie. "My aunt in Cleveland is sick, and I have to go with my parents for a week or so. This is the only time I had to show him my route before we leave in the morning."

I could not believe Boo thought this up so efficiently. I was usually the one to come up with the quick, good lies. One time I attempted to steal a Three Musketeers candy bar from the five-and-dime store. The manager, who had been watching us the entire time, grabbed me by the collar as Boo and I attempted to leave the store. He let Boo go because he did not take anything. I, on the other hand, was dragged to the office in the back of the store. The manager made me call my mother, who, when I left the house a half an hour before, was in my bedroom sewing clothing for my sisters. I knew she would sew for hours at a time. I let the phone ring a couple of times and, knowing she could not get to it quickly, started talking. The manager heard me say:

Hi mom, I stole a candy bar from the five-and-dime, and the manager caught me. I am in his office right now. Yes, okay. I understand. I placed the still ringing phone in its cradle without handing it back to the manager. It was just pure luck that he did not want to talk to her, or skill on my part for not letting him. When he asked me what she said, I told him she wanted me home right away. He let me go. Either he was on to my ruse, or believed my lie. I raced back to Watson Avenue to catch Boo to make sure he did not tell anybody what just happened. So when Kidwell caught us, it was Boo who came up with the quick lie, not me.

Kidwell did not know either of our parents, but he did know our names from the duck incident. He studied us intently, and we said nothing else.

"Well, when you're through, go home directly," he said. "We've had some vandalism in the park this summer. I don't want you boys to be tempted."

"Yes, sir," is all we said in return. We headed toward the fort, this time via the woods from Cherry Avenue.

Just like Teak-qua told us, when we awoke in the fort at seven o'clock, it was the morning after we left. Even though we were in the past for less than three days, we only missed a couple of hours in the present. We vowed never to worry about getting back late again. After our first cigarette, we rolled up our sleeping bags and headed back to my house. We stopped to feed the chickens in the fenced-in coop in our backyard. Boo picked his nose as I tossed corn to the chickens.

Okay, I admit I had a fascination with boogers when I was growing up. Something that was your own that grew right up your own nose was a real wonder of nature. I guess my fascination was also because it grossed out my sisters so much. Only grossed out was not a phrase popular in the fifties. I think the phrase we used a lot was "un-cool." You could chase away a nosy (no pun intended) sister and her friends just by inserting your finger, twisting, picking the biggest one, and waving the tip of your finger at them. Anyway, there is one booger story I recall that grossed out more than my sisters.

I guess Boo shared the same fascination with boogers. You could pick 'em, smear 'em on the walls, and stick 'em under your seat at church or school, where they crusted and waited for some poor schnook (hopefully a girl) to stick their hand on them. Then their brains would take a second or two before registering what that crusty thing was that just flaked off in their hand or got stuck under their fingernail. When they realized their worst fears, no amount of shaking or washing could get the thought that, momentarily, they had just touched what was once up someone's nose. A fresh one was the worst, but one that clung like a barnacle in waiting for a year or so was just as effective.

Every Easter my sisters and I, as a supplement to our Easter baskets, got baby chicks, or, as we called them, peepees. After we were done torturing them, they were placed in a small coop behind the garage and raised, until one day, if a dog didn't get in the coop first, they were taken to a farm to be raised, or so we were told. We then had chicken dinner every Sunday for a few weeks. As we got older, we caught on to the fact that we were eating the same chickens that we got for Easter. Nobody seemed to mind, since the cute little peepees got ugly as they matured. My job was to feed and water the chickens, which was kind of fun.

That morning Boo was experiencing especially good booger production and was inventing new ways to dispose of his catch, other than wiping them on his jeans. After a particularly good singing rendition of "Vios con Dios, My Booger," he gobbled one up. Even I thought that was a little un-cool. While I was feeding the chickens their daily corn and table scraps, Boo had other ideas. Yes, he dug one out and proffered it to one of the chickens. The chicken did, as Boo did earlier, gobble it up. We both thought that was cool, so he dug out another and fed it to the same chicken. I was done feeding the rest of the chickens, so we ambled on our way. I told no one and put the experience in the back of my mind, until one Sunday.

We always had a ham for Thanksgiving dinner and a turkey for Christmas. This was for two reasons, actually; one was my dad always got a turkey from his boss for Christmas and my grandfather did not like poultry. I tell you this because one Sunday, we had my grandparents for dinner, which, you may remember, was really lunch. Well, this Sunday we were having chicken for dinner at our house with my grandparents. My grandfather decided to eat a bit of the chicken, which shocked my mom. We were all sitting around the table eating.

The adults were talking, and my sisters and I were just eating and listening. I don't know why, but the vision of Boo feeding boogers to that chicken appeared suddenly. I was just thinking out loud when I held up a drumstick on the end of my fork and said, "I wonder if this is the one Boo fed the boogers to."

I heard two things: first the word "Giovanni" emanating from my mother, which meant I was in trouble. That was followed by forks all being put down simultaneously. I looked around with a shocked look on my face, wondering what I said to cause such a disgusted look on everyone's faces. I tried to take another bite of my drumstick, but was sent to my room instead. I have no idea what went on at the table in my absence, and to this day do not know what all the fuss was about. As far as I know, my grandfather never attempted to eat poultry again.

That night, all the kids in the neighborhood got together to play kickball in the street. We used to play softball until we put a ball through the neighbor's living room window. The rules for kickball were the same as softball, only a large rubber ball was rolled to the kicker instead of tossing a softball. The kicker then ran up and kicked the ball. An out was when the fielding team caught and threw the ball hitting a runner. It was safer to play than softball, and most of the smaller kids and non-athletic girls could play too. It tied up the street, but there were fewer cars back then.

Before the game, Boo and I were sitting on our bikes, head-in to the curb near David's house, talking to David and Mike, his big brother. Boo's cousin Judy was also with us and had an obvious crush on Mike. Mike was a tightwad and did not want to date anyone because it cost money. Trying to get Mike's attention, Judy wrapped her arms around a tree, saying—

"This is what I'm going to do to you, Mike." She then kissed the tree. Unfortunately, a large carpenter ant was in the same place as Judy's mouth. She backed away when she realized her tongue was sharing space with a wriggling critter. The sensation immediately caused her to expel her supper close to where my front wheel was parked.

At that same time, Bobbie-Lou and Linda were riding their bikes down the street toward us. Like David and Mike, Linda was one of the few kids on the block our age without a nickname. Linda, in my opinion, was ugly. Bobbie-Lou and Linda lived two doors apart on the same side of the street, and they were inseparable. Linda was taller than most boys, considered not very attractive, and had no discernable shape; but then next to Bobbie-Lou, other girls looked ugly and shapeless, even by our juvenile standards. Linda had an upturned nose that stuck up so high you could almost see her brains by looking up her nostrils. She wore horned-rimmed glasses, which probably was the only choice for girls in the fifties. Her ears were large and stuck out from her head. My dad used to say she looked like a taxicab going down the street with both rear doors open. The only reason we paid any attention to her was that she hung out with Bobbie-Lou.

As they approached on the same side of the street where we were watching Judy soil the curb, I stuck the rear end of my bike out to avoid the protein spill. Instead of stopping, or at least swerving (Linda was on the outside of her), Bobbie-Lou ran smack-dab into my rear wheel. Both of us went sprawling. I did not sustain any injuries, but she skinned her knee on the pavement. She was not injured that badly, but was crying.

While she inspected the damage to her knee, I stared at her. It was amazing how much she looked like Nightstar. In a few minutes, she got up on her bike and, giving me a sour look, rode away with Linda. She must have thought I stuck my bike wheel out on purpose. Every one of the boys on Watson had a crush on her at one time or another. It was my turn this summer. If she thought the accident was my fault, my chances of ever currying her favor were lost forever.

Her injuries did not keep her out of the kickball game that evening; however, she played with a large Band-Aid on the scraped knee. She must have told her father what happened, because when I was sitting on the curb, awaiting my turn "at bat," he came out of his house and told me that if I *ever hurt her again*, he would *cut my ears off*. When the others later asked me what he said that made me turn white, I told them, leaving off the part about hurting her again. They were all puzzled by the statement, but he became Mr. Cut-Your-Ears-Off after that.

Boo and I did not sleep in the fort that night. I found out later that he and David sat up on the bank behind Bobbie-Lou's house to see if they could catch her undressing through her upstairs bedroom window. What they did see was Bobbie-Lou's mother doing the striptease through the first-floor bedroom window. They suspected that she knew they were there, and played along. When she got to the part where they were sure she was going to take off her bra, she pulled the window shade down, depriving them of a their first real peep show.

The next night we were at the fort. When we woke up to Teak-qua's chanting, we were ready with a lot of questions.

"Why didn't we have to kill anyone on our last trip?" I asked.

"We had fun hunting, but what was the purpose?" Boo added. "Are we going back there?"

"I wanted you to see how simple life was for them," Teak-qua responded. "Were they not a gentle people?"

"Yes," I smiled, remembering my dream with Nightstar. "Can we go back again?"

"You will go back tonight," Teak-qua said. "But be prepared for seeing some frightening scenes. It will give you the courage to avenge."

"Will Nightstar get hurt?" I asked.

"You will see," Teak-qua replied. "You will see."

"Are we going back where we left off?" Boo asked.

"It will be in the winter when you return," Teak-qua said.

"Damn, it was cold when we were there," Boo said. "They had to give us bearskins to keep warm. Should we take coats with us this time?"

"As before, you will be given what you need," Teak-qua said.

"How long will we be gone this time?" I asked.

"As always, just one night," he said. "But in the past, long enough to avenge. Now you must go. Moonbeam awaits. This time, she will be at the place with the water pump."

"If you mean Liberty Park, that's good, because we had trouble with Kidwell last night," I said, but Teak-qua had resumed chanting and smoking his pipe.

Boo and I got up from our sleeping bags. We took the canvas bag and our BB guns, leaving Teak-qua to his pleasures.

Liberty Park was across the street from South Liberty School, the grade school Boo and I attended. The park had a water well with an old-fashioned hand pump. The pump was inside an open shelter, just off the highway on the top of the hill leading down into the park. The cast-iron pump was painted green, but had a good amount of rust on it. That did not deter us from using it. One person would pump the handle and any number of us would cup our hands and drink the cool, metallic-tasting water that issued forth from deep in the earth. The pump is still there, but not working, since, I am sure, the water is no longer considered safe. Back then, it sure tasted good on a hot summer day, especially after a long bike ride or a game of softball. My grandmother, in later years when she lived across the street from us, used to walk to the well with a wheeled cart and bring back gallon jugs of the water. She would not drink the city water and even made foul-tasting coffee with the well water. She lived to be a hundred and three years old, so the water must have been okay.

At the bottom of the hill was a poorly kept baseball diamond. There were no supervised sports as there were at Silver Park, and it was a bit farther from Watson Avenue; therefore, we did not frequent this park as much. One time Boo did run around the ball diamond at night in nothing but his underpants while Bart held a flashlight on him. Boo did this on a dare, but not until he convinced Bart and his brother to give him all the change they had. It amounted to a dollar. Another dare that summer had Boo riding a Vespa motor scooter around the neighborhood block at night in his underpants. This earned him another dollar. From then on he was known as Anything-For-a-Buck Boo.

On the way to the park, we passed Mike's Warehouse. We stopped at the trash bin at the rear of Mike's store and found an apple and carrot that had not met Mike's strict adherence to quality. We carried them with us for our favorite horse

As we entered the park down the hill, we spotted Moonbeam at the far side of the ball field. She appeared and disappeared as a curtain of clouds moved across the moon, now waning after the full moon of the past couple of nights. When the moonlight gave her presence away, Moonbeam looked like a silver statue. As we approached, she saw us and shook her head up and down. She then walked across the field to meet us. She gladly munched the apple and carrot as we hoisted each other up on her back.

Moonbeam took her usual gallop across the field behind the park. Boo and I rode straight up as we had learned on the previous trips. As Moonbeam circled higher, we looked down at the little town we called home, Mike's warehouse, South Liberty School, and Liberty Park. After the spectacular aerial view, we headed west through the blur of stars and moonlight for whatever awaited us. Only we were not prepared for the horror we would witness.

We arrived at the Bear River Indian encampment, which did not look much different than when we left it two of our days before. All of the trees were bare. The sun was low in the west, and campfires were burning. It was noticeably colder than on our last trip. There was some excitement in the camp, but not from our arrival. As we left Moonbeam to graze with the other horses, Touches-Bear noticed us and came out to greet us. He stopped in at his teepee momentarily, and Nightstar was soon on her way with our bearskin coats. She was smiling at me, not with just her mouth, but with her entire face. She had the pendant tied around her neck and held it to her heart when she saw me.

"Someone is glad to see you," Boo said, casting a wary glance at me. "Are you sure that it was just a sucking bus?"

"That's succubus, and I'm not so sure now," I responded, amazed that Boo had remembered the word. Succubus was one of those sort-of-dirty words that once you looked up, you never forgot.

"How are you, my warriors?" Touches-Bear asked.

"We're okay," Boo said. "What is all the excitement about?"

"Chief Hunts Bear is angry with his sons and some of our young warriors," he responded. "They went on a raid of the white settlers in the valley, soon after you left. We are now preparing for battle."

"Why did they do that?" Boo asked.

"The settlers control almost all of the fertile lands," he continued. "They also are controlling the water. They do not respect the land and water, fouling both. The warriors took matters into their own hands, and now there are soldiers coming from the west to avenge the white man."

"Can you hide in the mountains?" I asked.

"We cannot move the entire village in time, so we will stay and fight," Touches-Bear said. "We will wait on the eastern bank for them to attack."

"When will that happen?" Boo asked.

"The soldiers are camped about half a day away," Touches-Bear said. "They will probably attack sometime tomorrow."

"Can we help?" I asked.

"All preparations have been made. If you want, you can stay and fight with us tomorrow. We can use all the guns and ammunition available. Our supplies are low because of the raids the warriors made."

"We'll stay," Boo and I said in unison.

We followed Touches-Bear to the campfire in front of his tent. Nightstar was there, as well as some other women, all cooking meat on the fire. As we approached, the other women looked at me and then at Nightstar and started giggling. I was confused by this greeting and started to flush in spite of the cold air. Night was fast approaching, revealing a blanket of bright stars in the cloudless moonless night. Boo and I sat down by the fire and were presented with meat and flatbread. I was not all that hungry and picked restlessly at the meat.

Boo was talking to Touches-Bear as I felt someone's presence on my right. Nightstar sat down next to me and I smiled at her. She moved in a little closer, our bearskins touching.

"How are you?" I asked.

"I am fine, now that you are here," she said. "Thank you for giving me the stone. I will wear it the rest of my life."

I felt the rush of blood to my face again, as I know I must have turned several shades of red. I turned my face back toward the fire and held up my hands, fingers up, palms turned out, to catch the radiant heat. My heart seemed like it was trying to beat its way out of my chest as she grabbed my right hand and held it in hers. The touch was warm, gentle, and soft.

"When I was here before," I started, in a cracked voice. I swallowed hard and started over. "When I was here before, did we kiss in the tent at night, or was that just a dream?"

"We did kiss," she said. "It was my first time, and I think it was yours too."

"It was my first time," I lied, blushing again.

"I enjoyed the kissing and hugging and can't wait to do it again. My heart has been aching since you have been gone."

"I have thought of nothing but that night and of you," I lied, not knowing what else to say. I did not want to tell her she reminded me of Bobbie-Lou.

She smiled and moved in closer to me, putting her arm around mine. The light from the fire illuminated her face in a yellowish tint. There was an internal brightness to her eyes, which were also reflecting the dancing flames of the campfire. The stone she had on was on the outside for all to see. It caught the light from the flames and seemed to dance like her eyes.

At that moment it seemed like the whole camp got up at once. Almost all were moving into their respective tents. The dogs were put out to stand guard. Nightstar stood up, pulling on my hand. As I stood up, I could see Moonbeam down by the river with the other horses. She stood out, shining in the light given off by the stars. As I turned to go toward the tent, Moonbeam looked in my direction and shook her head up and down, as if waving good night to me.

As we entered the tent this time, Nightstar led me over to the bed we occupied last time. Boo looked at me with this "shame, shame" nod of his head from right to left and back again. I was again red in the face as Nightstar pulled me down to lay beside her. We undressed under the bearskin blanket, sharing each other's warmth. She had nothing on but the pendant. Touches-Bear and his wife retired to their bed without even a glance in our direction. Soon all were snoring away except Nightstar and me. We were wriggling in each other's arms, as if trying to get closer. She looked up to me and I bent my head down, kissing her gently on her open mouth. We both started breathing hard.

She grabbed me with both arms around my back and pulled me closer to her. She put her head against the hollow in my neck and started to breathe normally again after a minute or two. I moved my arms down around her back, while she clung to mine. I could feel the stone between us connecting our hearts. I rested my head next to hers and we both fell into a deep sleep.

I awoke to Boo shaking me on the shoulder. Nightstar and I had released each other during the night, but she was still lying beside me.

"Hey," Boo said in a rough whisper. "Wake up, Moonbeam is trying to get our attention."

"Wha', wha'?" I asked, still in a sleep-induced stupor. "What's going on?"

"It must be time to go," Boo said. "Moonbeam woke me up, and she's getting agitated."

"Oh, okay," I said, rubbing my eyes with my free hand. I slowly pulled my left hand out from under Nightstar, who gave a sigh and rolled over, her back toward me.

"What time is it?" I asked, sitting up and putting my pants and shirt on. I still had on my socks, so all I had to do was put on my shoes and lace them up.

"It's one o'clock," Boo said, squinting at the luminous hands of Roy.

"That's too early to go back," I said. "We usually stay until three our time." I looked over toward Moonbeam's head, which was halfway through the tent door. I gave her a look as if to ask what was up. She just nodded her head up and down, and let out a snort. I stood up, putting on my bearskin coat. Boo already had his on. Moonbeam backed out of the tent. We followed her. No one was stirring in the camp but the dogs. They only gave us a glance and then went about their business of guarding.

Moonbeam nodded toward her back, indicating to us we were supposed to get on.

"I guess we're going back early this time," Boo responded to my earlier comment. "We haven't done anything again, if that is the case. I wonder why Teak-qua sent us this time? Just so you could see your girlfriend, I guess."

"Bite me!" I said, in response. "Just bite me." I put my foot in Boo's cupped hands and hoisted myself up on Moonbeam, pulling Boo up behind me. Our breath was condensing in large, billowy clouds in the cold, morning air. Moonbeam's was doing the same, only her clouds were so large they almost engulfed all three of us.

Moonbeam turned toward the east, took three good strides, and was airborne. This time, there were no streaking stars. We were not traveling through time, but were just circling, gaining altitude.

We said nothing as we circled ever higher. The sun was coming up; at least we could see it at the altitude we were riding Moonbeam. The earth below us was still dark. We could just make out the Indian camp far below. As the light spread down the far mountains and across the earth, we could see a group of men. They were mounted soldiers heading west toward the camp. Although it was still dark at the camp, we could see the Indians scurrying about behind the eastern embankment of Beaver Creek, no doubt aroused by the guard dogs.

"What time do you think it is here?" I asked.

"About six o'clock," Boo responded. "What do you think's going on down there?"

"I don't know, but it looks like the soldiers are going to attack the camp," I said, turning to answer Boo. "I guess that's why Moonbeam wanted us out of there."

As I turned back to look down at the camp, the first wave of soldiers charged. We could see flashes of light from the guns on both sides. The sound of the battle was muted at our higher altitude. We watched as about two dozen soldiers were cut down in the charge. They pulled back and began to regroup.

About ten minutes later, the soldiers split up and began to encircle the camp. Surrounded and outnumbered, the Indians were getting shot at from 360 degrees. We could see women and children being hit by gunfire, as well as the braves. To us, it was as though we were watching a Saturday afternoon matinee at the Strand Theater, only this time it was real, or a bad dream.

The battle ensued for a good hour until all the firing was going into the camp. None was returned. The Indians had run out of ammunition, and were scattering into the dense willows in and around the camp. The soldiers then commenced to massacre anyone they could find. They rode through the camp with their revolvers, shooting anyone not white. They also rode into the willows and shot the ones they could find.

Moonbeam circled lower until we could see the faces of the soldiers, who were intent on not leaving anyone alive. They proceeded to rape any woman they happened across, and bashed in the heads of the wounded and dying women and children. They were so intent on what they were doing they failed to notice two horrified teenagers on horseback circling above them. Our tears plummeted to the earth, only to evaporate before touching the busy soldiers. We were close enough to hear one of the men call out the name of the colonel in charge. The name was Connor.

When we thought the carnage was over, the soldiers set fire to the village and gathered all the food stores they could find. They left with the Shoshone horses, the wounded and dead soldiers, and the supplies taken from the Indians. As they moved toward the south, Moonbeam came back to earth.

We did not dismount at first. In the early afternoon sun, Moonbeam walked around the destruction. Boo and I looked in disbelief at what the soldiers left behind. There were mutilated bodies everywhere. We could not find a single person alive. Just as I was about to ask Boo if he'd seen Nightstar, we came upon her body. I jumped down from Moonbeam, while Boo stayed on the horse. I knelt down and tried to touch her, but was afraid. Her head was nearly split in two, and blood was everywhere.

I almost threw up, but was too disgusted. Anger was boiling up inside me like a pressure cooker. I noticed a piece of rawhide sticking out of her clenched right hand. I bent down and gently pried her fingers apart. Inside was the pendant. It was amazing the soldiers did not take it from her. She must have realized they would, and at the last moment took it off and held it tightly in her hand, hoping I would return and find it. I retrieved the pendant, kissed it, and put it around my neck.

Moonbeam nudged me, urging me to remount. Reluctantly, I got on behind Boo. As we lifted away from what had been a peaceful Indian settlement, the tears started to flow again. The tears continued as the stars turned into streaks. Moonbeam was taking us back to the present, where we could think about our next trip and, hopefully, revenge.

Seven

When I awoke this time, I pulled my knees to my chest and tried to fight the tears, but they came, slowly at first and then steadily. I was sobbing quietly as Boo awoke.

"Was the massacre we witnessed a dream?" I asked between sobs. I lowered my forehead onto my knees, somewhat embarrassed to let Boo see me in tears.

"If it was, I dreamed it too," Boo responded. "All I want to do is kill the bastards that did that to Bobbie-Lou."

"Did what to me?" asked a female voice from outside our fort.

Boo and I both snapped our heads toward the front of the fort as Bobbie-Lou's demure face appeared in the opening. I quickly rubbed the tears from my eyes.

"Have you got a flashlight, so we can see to come in?" Bobbie-Lou asked.

Boo grabbed for and turned on the light, shining it to the front of the cave. I realized I was still wearing the pendant dangling from my neck. I took it off and put it in my pocket.

"Who's we?" I asked, although I had an idea it would be Linda.

"Turn the light away from our eyes," Linda said. Her face then appeared, contrasting with Bobbie-Lou's beauty. Turning to Bobbie-Lou, she said, "Umbday oybays."

"Oybays ancay ebay upidstay," Bobbie-Lou responded, and they both giggled. The two of them reverted to pig Latin when they wanted to say something for their ears only. When they spoke that way to each other, it was so fast and the response so quick, we "umbday oybays" seldom understood. They must have practiced a lot to get good at it.

Boo had moved the light to the side, and they both bent down and entered our fort. Mugsy appeared at the entrance with his rock in his mouth.

"What were you talking about?" Bobbie-Lou asked again.

"How long have you been spying on us?" I asked, trying to change the subject. Linda squatted down on Boo's sleeping bag. I thought Bobbie-Lou would come over and sit on mine, but, as my heart raced, she sat down next to Linda. Mugsy came in and sat on my bag, looking up at me, slobber dripping from the sides of his mouth and down his rock. He set the rock down, wanting me to pick it up and toss it.

"Long enough to hear you talk about somebody doing something to me in a dream," she said. "Do you have any cigarettes?" I reached for the pack of unfiltered Chesterfields that was lying on the table and handed them to her.

"So what was your dream all about?" she continued. She pulled out two cigarettes and handed one to Linda. Boo was quick to strike a Blue Tip and offered them a light. I was jealous as hell when Bobbie-Lou cupped her hand around Boo's hand as she took a drag. Boo then handed the lit match to Linda, who lit her own.

"He'd tell you, but he'd have to cut your ears off," Boo said. Boo and I laughed at his obvious mimicking of her father's comment to me. Bobbie-Lou looked at me and smiled. I thought I must have been forgiven for the bike incident the night before. I found out later that David told her I was just trying to dodge the puke. Boo took a cigarette of his own and handed the pack back to me. We both struck our own Blue Tip and lit our cigarettes.

"How many times have you been here?" I asked, referring to the fort. I was now feeling much better, now that Bobbie-Lou, aka Nightstar, was obviously alive and well. Maybe it was just a dream Boo and I had. I picked up Mugsy's rock and tossed it out of the cave. It rolled down the hill with a joyful Mugsy scampering off in hot pursuit. We were not aware that "the girls" knew about our fort.

"Two times," Linda said with a smirk, blowing a puff of smoke toward the entrance.

"Maybe it was three," Bobbie-Lou added. She blew a haze of blue-white smoke from her cigarette toward no one in particular. I wished she had blown the smoke in my direction. I read somewhere that such a gesture meant she cared for me, but it was not to be today.

"We saw the bones," Linda said, nodding toward the rear of the fort. "Why did you put them there?"

"We didn't," Boo said. "They were there when we dug the dirt out. They belong to an Indian."

Linda let out a shriek of laughter, almost dropping her cigarette.

"An Indian," she said. "What was his name, Tonto?"

Boo was about to say *no, Teak-qua,* when I interrupted with a "none of your business" answer. Mugsy returned with the rock in his mouth, and some dirt and grass clinging to the side. He promptly trotted over to me and dropped the rock at my side. I ignored him while I took a drag. None of us were inhaling.

Bobbie-Lou was starring at me inquisitively, like she knew the whole story. I was a little ashamed that she might be able to tell I had been crying over her dream twin being killed and mutilated.

"There is a movie at Mount Union," I blurted out. "Do you want to go with us?" All three of them looked at me surprised.

"What movie is it?" Linda asked, flicking an ash in my direction. I wasn't sure what that gesture meant. "I don't want to see a cowboy movie," she continued. Now I was in trouble, because I had no idea what the movie was. Back then, movies changed weekly, and unless you paid attention, you would have no idea. Boo and I almost always went to the Strand Theater rather than Mount Union. The Strand was much further away.

The Strand always had Westerns, sci-fi, or, one summer, 3-D. The 3-D movies were incredible, but after watching the same movie two or three times, we got terrible headaches. I guess that is why there are no 3-D movies playing on a regular basis anymore.

"*Blackboard Jungle*," Bobbie-Lou said, coming to my rescue. "It has Glenn Ford and Sidney Poitier in it. Sure, we'll go. Is this a date?"

"No, we'll just go together," I responded. I didn't think I could come up with two quarters for myself, let alone a date. I picked up the rock and tossed it out of the fort again. This time farther than the last. Mugsy followed in pursuit of his treasure.

"We'll buy the popcorn," Boo added, with a puff of smoke. He was now wishing it was his idea. "Who's Sidney Potter?"

"It's not Potter, you idiot," Linda said. "Poitier." She pronounced his name *pwa-tea-a*, closing her eyes and lifting her face up as she said it. I looked up her nose, and I swear could see her brains. "He's a Negro, and very good-looking."

"Ya mean a nigger?" said Boo with a smirk.

"Well, we can't go today," Linda said, obviously ignoring the racial slur. "We have plans." As she finished the sentence, she stubbed out her cigarette on the dirt floor of the fort.

"Tomorrow afternoon will be fine," I said.

"Okay," Bobbie-Lou said, and stubbed out her cigarette. She and Linda got up as if on cue. "We'll see you later."

"Say hello to your Indian friend. Et'slay ogay," Linda added.

As they left, Mugsy trotted up to the entrance of the fort with the rock in his mouth. He looked toward me and then toward his owner, deciding on the latter.

"Where did you come up with that idea?" Boo asked as soon as he decided they were out of our hearing range.

"I don't know, it just came to me," I responded. "You didn't have to tell them about Teak-qua's bones. If we told them the whole story, they would just make fun of us, especially Linda. Have you got the money?"

"Yeah, I got some, but not enough" Boo said. His cigarette was burning down to a short butt. He took a paper clip off the table and attached the butt to it. He took another long drag, holding the paper clip so he could smoke as much of the cigarette as possible. He decided the cigarette was spent after the last drag, so he removed the paper clip and put it in one of the bags we used for our trips to the past. We each now had our own canvas bag for the trips.

"Don't want to waste these cigarettes," he said in response to my inquisitive glance. I later learned that was how a marijuana joint was smoked; only the paper clip was called a roach clip.

"I think I got enough for the movie, but I may have to hit my sister's piggy bank for popcorn money."

My baby sister's piggy bank was a source of emergency money for me. She had a large, blue, plastic piggy bank that was kept on the bottom shelf of an end table in our living room. Whenever my grandfather would visit, he would give her his spare change. She was six years younger than I was, so I suppose the preferential treatment was warranted, but I felt a twinge of jealousy when she had all that money and I had none. The bottom of the pig had a twist-off access hole. When I was sure no one was around, I would lie on my back and twist it off. I could then stick a pencil in the hole and flip out enough money to tide me over until the next time I got the urge. In the aggregate, I don't think I took more than a few dollars worth, but the guilt still bothers me, even though I confessed it as stealing. The sin of stealing was always good for a rosary or two, depending on the amount of the theft.

"How are we going to get revenge on those assholes that did that to Bobbie-Lou?" I asked. Boo gave me a "shush" signal with his right index finger to his mouth. Then he crept toward the front of the fort and peeked around the corner. He then stepped outside and looked on the roof. Satisfied that they were gone, he ducked back in.

"First of all, that was Bobbie-Lou who was just here, not the girl in the past," he responded. "As far as getting rid of Colonel Connor, I guess we'll just play it by ear like we did last time, or ask Teak-qua. Now, let's go cut some grass so we can afford to go to the movies. If we get enough, maybe we can treat them and afford some jujubes too, and you won't have to rob your sister's piggy bank."

I thought treating the "girls" was a great idea. Maybe it would help the guilt I also felt for causing Bobbie-Lou to hit my bike. I liked jujubes better than popcorn anyway. They were so hard, it was like eating bullets, but they were so tasty. They also were good for bouncing off someone's head from the balcony at the Strand.

Boo and I cut grass to earn enough money to do the simple things we wanted. Boo and I had only a couple of yards of our own. David, on the other hand, was the entrepreneur. He had at least ten yards. He also had a self-propelled, power lawn mower he bought with his paper route money. Sometimes when the grass was growing faster than he could cut it, or when he was going on vacation, he asked for our help. With his grass and paper route money, David bought his own 1956 Chevy as soon as he turned sixteen.

David was strong for his short stature. He got his strength from wrestling with his bigger and stronger, older brother Mike. David was good-looking. All of the girls on Watson had a crush on him at one time or another. He was only a month or two older than I was, but because he was born before the school year was out, he was a grade ahead of me. He had blond hair and had no fat on him. He was always playing hard or working.

One summer, Boo and David took booze, a little at a time, from their father's liquor bottles. It was such a small amount each time, their fathers never noticed. At the end of the summer, they had a quart mason jar full of whiskey, gin, and vodka stored in David's attic. It was a Saturday afternoon when they decided to drink the stolen booze. An hour later, the jar was empty. It was time to deliver the afternoon paper, and they were smashed. They folded and stuffed the papers for both their routes at the L&J's Drugstore. When done, they decided to do both routes together. David would peddle along the street, while Boo sat on the handlebars and tossed the papers onto the porches along the routes.

They were still drunk when I heard the paper plop on our porch. I went out to get it, and witnessed David running smack into the back end of a car. Boo went flying onto the roof of the car and rolled out into the street. David wound up upside down on the trunk of the car, still holding onto his bike, which flipped with him. I watched in amazement as they both started laughing like nothing had happened. David's bike was so damaged, they had to finish their routes on foot, stumbling and laughing the entire time. They later got calls from people who did not receive their papers. Both of them had to spend their own money to buy more papers to deliver.

David and Boo did not stop drinking after that episode. They got hold of some beer from a friend and went driving in David's '56 Chevy. Coming back into town, they took an S-curve at better than ninety miles per, with a cop car going in the opposite direction. To get rid of evidence, and to try and give the cop car a flat tire, they tossed the empty beer bottles behind them, smashing them on the road. It was late and very dark that night, so they were able to get back to Watson Avenue, but the cop was close behind. David kept his car in the neighbor's garage adjacent to my bedroom window. I heard the Chevy tires screech around the corner. When I put the book down I was reading and looked out my bedroom window, I saw Boo open the garage door and David drive in the garage. Boo shut the door behind him, and David exited through the garage side door.

As they headed up the street toward Boo's house, I saw the police cruiser stop and talk to them. I found out the next day, that the cop was looking for the "possibly blue, older model Chevy" that he had been chasing. "Nope, we haven't seen it," David said.

The grass was not growing fast enough for David to ask us for help, so that afternoon, Boo and I hitched our push mowers up to the back of our bikes and rode to our own lawn-cutting jobs. We were hot and sweaty when we were done, so it was off to LaNave's swimming pool for the rest of the afternoon.

LaNave's was a private swimming pool on Route 62. We went there as often as we could afford. Since we got paid five dollars for the grass cutting, we had enough for a day of swimming and the promised movies with the girls. We would spend the entire afternoon at the pool, swimming and diving. Sometimes we got lucky and retrieved coins from the pool bottom. The pool was octagonal, with the perimeter being shallow and the center twelve foot deep. A low and high diving platform jutted out from one end. We would dive from the low platform. We saw too many belly flops made from the high platform, so we just jumped rather than dived from it. Neither one of us wanted the embarrassment of a poor high dive not to mention the sting and red belly that would stay with us the rest of the day. They had food at the pool, but it was too expensive for us unless we found a lot of money on the bottom.

Having exhausted ourselves with work and play, when it was time to go to sleep in the fort that night, we both fell promptly to sleep. We both had to be awakened by Teak-qua at one thirty. As I wiped the sleep from my eyes, Boo started to get dressed and was already asking Teak-qua questions.

"How are we going to get even with Colonel Connor?" he asked first.

"This is up to you," Teak-qua said. "You will find the necessary resources in the pouches you carry."

"Do we need to off anyone else?" Boo continued.

"This too will be determined by the circumstances," Teak-qua said.

"Damn it!" Boo said. "Can't you give us a straight answer for a change?"

I shuddered at the brashness of Boo's comments, but felt similarly. I made a mental sign of the cross for Boo's sake. Teak-qua said nothing at first, and continued to smoke his pipe.

"You are warriors," he said, in a calm voice after a long pause. "I trust your judgment, and since I cannot be there with you, I leave you to your own devices. You saw what happened; you felt the pain; you will make the correct choices when the time comes."

I could feel the lack of patience in Teak-qua's voice. I needed to ask him a question, but waited a long moment before I dared to say anything.

"Sorry," Boo said. "I'm tired after a long day."

"Teak-qua," I interjected. He said nothing, took a long drag on his pipe, and looked at me.

"Is it possible to go back and be with Nightstar?" I continued. "I mean, can Moonbeam take us back to before the massacre, so I can see her again? I really like her."

"She lives in the one you call Bobbie-Lou," Teak-qua said. "My people believe in living again after death. Nightstar is in her second life."

"But does Bobbie-Lou know this?" I probed.

"It is enough that you know," Teak-qua said, looking directly at me. "Now be off, my warriors. Moonbeam and another adventure await you." Boo and I grabbed our BB guns and canvas bags and headed for the park.

When we arrived in the past, Moonbeam took us over the site of the Shoshone camp. We were low enough to view the bodies. There were wolves eating the remains, while crows picked over what the wolves did not want. I was feeling anger like I never felt before.

"Hurry up, Moonbeam," I urged. "I don't want to see anymore of this."

"How many days do you think have gone by?" Boo asked.

"I don't know," I responded. "Maybe two or three. There's not much we can do about this. I don't see any soldiers' bodies down there."

Moonbeam gained some altitude and headed south. Soon we came upon several tents, some wooden buildings, and some other buildings under construction. The completed buildings were in a row at the northeast side of the encampment. These buildings were smaller and looked like individual houses or office buildings. The northwest and southeast sides had completed structures mixed in with some incomplete, framed-out buildings. These larger structures must have been barracks. The buildings were in a grassy area surrounding a gravel-covered, dirt parade ground about the size of two football fields laid side by side. Creek beds ran along the back sides of the larger structures, and behind the office buildings. Another row of small houses was set back away from the office buildings. Beyond that was a hill rising up to two smaller buildings on either side of a barn-like structure. A sign came into view indicating this was Camp Douglas. There was activity at the camp, but no one was looking toward the sky. Moonbeam took advantage of some cloud cover as we circled the camp. Boo and I took some mental notes of the locations of what must have been the key structures.

"Moonbeam," I said. "Can you set down and walk us through the camp as if we belonged there?" She responded with a nod of the head.

"What are you, crazy?" Boo asked. "You gotta be nuts to just march right into the middle of those soldiers. What if they come at us?"

"I'm not worried," I responded, although I was a little concerned. "I think they're too busy to notice us. Besides, if there is trouble, Moonbeam can get us out of it. Can't you, Moonbeam?" She whinnied, shaking her head up and down. Taking a downward angle and heading toward what looked like the back of the camp, Moonbeam set down like a feather falling toward earth. She then just trotted toward the center of the camp. Most of the soldiers were living in tents on the U-shaped quadrangle. The officers seemed to be occupying the buildings set back on the northeast side.

One building had a crudely made sign declaring it to be HQ, or headquarters. The soldiers were too busy carrying on their daily routines to pay us much attention. Some were marching in the graveled area; others were working on the construction of the barracks. There were also a few women about. They didn't look like very respectable women to me, but then I was not experienced in those matters. Moonbeam trotted around the rear of the HQ building.

Behind it were two outhouses, the signs on each indicating they were for officers only. Above the outhouses was a slight rise. Moonbeam climbed the rise. From there we could see almost all of the camp.

"Why don't we just sit up on this hill and start shooting these assholes?" Boo asked. "We could wait until morning when the sun is at our back."

"That's too much like a Western movie," I countered. "I don't think we could get away with it. There are too many soldiers, and we may not get Colonel Connor. I want to get him for sure. Let's get away from here and think about it.

When we got to the cover of some nearby piney woods, we got off Moonbeam and sat down on the needle-covered earth. I opened my bag and looked inside. Boo did the same with his. I dumped out the contents; Boo did not.

"We have some of this rocket fuel and carbide pellets," I said. "Good thing the ground is dry, or we'd have stinky acetylene gas right now. Your farts are bad enough."

"Screw you," was Boo's response. "I got even less. Some string, paper clips, and a half-empty pack of Chesterfields." Just then he cut a fart, a loud one that stunk worse than the acetylene gas. I backed away. Moonbeam let out a whinny and backed away too.

"That was a good one," Boo said with a shit-eating grin. "I shoulda lit that baby."

"Yeah, and the soldiers could just follow the blast and smoke to locate our bodies," I said, sneering and holding my nose.

We knew farts burned because we did just that in Boo's house one rainy day when his parents and sister were gone. It was a regular fart fest. I could not use the word fart at home, but my dad solved that problem with an Italian word. He used the word skudida. Whether that was an Italian word, or something he made up, I had no way of knowing.

All four of us, Boo, Skubini, Dave, and I were sitting in Boo's living room smoking. Boo, in his dad's favorite chair, cut one, and we all laughed. David said that Jimmy, another paperboy our age, cut one near a gas furnace in the basement, where they folded papers for their routes in the winter, and flames shot out from his ass. The rest of us said bullshit, just as Boo let another one rip.

"I'll light the next one," Boo said. "For a buck." So we all chipped in to see if farts really did burn. Boo stripped to his jockeys, and we all waited. We could tell he was straining, and in a minute, he got into fart-lighting position by raising his knees up to his head, holding his legs against him with one hand, and lighting the lighter with the other. We all bent down, at a respectable distance, to get a look at Boo's crotch. His underpants were stretched tight, with the Zippo's yellow flame flickering near his butt. When he cut this one, a bluish streak of burning skudida went up the middle of his pants. We all howled in excitement.

David then cut one and so he stripped to his shorts and sat back on the couch. In a couple of minutes, as we were discussing the color and size of Boo's flame, David started to grunt, assumed the position, and lit his Zippo in anticipation, so we bent down to watch. David's skudida was bigger than Boo's, or his ass was smaller, but the flame was definitely larger than Boo's. This sent me, Skubini, and Boo rolling on the floor, our sides splitting. Boo jumped up and got into position on his dad's chair. He lit another one, which outdid David's.

I did not have a skudida in me, but Skubini wanted to join the club. He was going to try to light a skudida whether he had one or not. He stripped, assumed the position, and started to push and grunt. When he lit his lighter, the rest of us just bent down, but not too close. Skubini's butt, being somewhat bigger than Boo's or David's, was not a pretty sight. He then let out a grunt, but it wasn't a skudida that came out, it was a turd. Not a solid turd either, but a wet one that went right trough his pants. Like a dog marking its territory, Skubini forever branded the Zippo as his. After that, if we did not have a light for our smoke, and Skubini had his lighter to offer, we did not smoke. There was no way we wanted the "Stinko Zippo" waved in front of our noses. Skubini's little accident ruined the game for the rest of us. As he went home to change his pants, David and I left too. We did, however, have confirmed proof, that skudidas burned.

Boo's fart gave me an idea.

"Hey, why don't we drop some carbide tablets in one of the crappers? Then when that asshole Connor comes out to take a shit, we can light a match and blow him up, just like we do those tin cans."

"We gotta have water to make it work," Boo added.

"Not if he takes a piss while he's poopin'. Let's piss on a piece of the carbide to see if it reacts just like it does with water," I suggested. I tossed a piece of the carbide a little ways from where we were sitting. Boo got up, went over to it, unzipped his pants, and pissed on it. It bubbled up just as if it were immersed in water.

"Well, that works," I exclaimed.

"How are we gonna light it without gettin' ourselves blowed up?" Boo had a good point. If a small can blew sky high, splattering mud all over us, then an outhouse full of acetylene would wipe out the person lighting it at the same time, or at least cover said person with shit.

"I know," Boo continued. "Let's light a cigarette and toss it at the outhouse. We could do it from up on the hill."

"We might miss," I countered. "A cigarette is hard to throw accurately, and might not be hot enough. If we could light a chunk of rocket fuel and toss that, it would do the job better."

"Or," Boo continued, "we could attach a paper clip to it and slide it down a length of string."

"It might burn through the string."

"Use two paper clips and dangle it further down," Boo argued. "Let's try it out first."

So we attached a length of string to the bottom of a tree and stretched it out. I got on Moonbeam, and Boo handed me the string. He made a hook out of the paper clip and looped it around a small piece of rocket fuel. He then fashioned another paper clip to that and handed it to me. I hooked it over the string, pulled it tight, and let it slide down the piece of string unlit. Boo then got it back to me, and

I lit it. Moonbeam let out a little surprise of a jerk, but stayed steady. I let the lit fuel slide down the string. It worked. The fuel did not burn the string and stayed lit all the way to the tree trunk. We had our delivery system.

"When are we gonna do this?" Boo asked.

"First thing in the morning. We have all night to prepare. Moonbeam, wake us up just before dawn." She gave a nod. Boo and I lay down for a nap.

I had a dream. I was with Nightstar. We were walking hand in hand, only we were younger. It wasn't the 1950s. It was earlier, much earlier. From the history books I read in school, I guessed it was around the early 1900s. We were in a town. It looked like a town from back east, maybe Philadelphia or Boston. There were horses and carriages everywhere. It was noisy. We were oblivious to our surroundings, as if in a cocoon, protected from the dangers of the world. But the scenery was changing. Every block we walked, the time was advancing. I looked at my watch. The hands were spinning very fast. The minute hand was a blur, and the hour hand was like the second hand on a stopwatch.

I looked over at Nightstar. She was smiling at me. A smile that made my heart melt and my knees buckle. She squeezed my hand and held me up. She was mouthing something to me, trying to be heard through the cacophony of sound from all around us. At last I was able to understand the words. She was telling me that she was all right. That she was fine. There were no scars on her from the mutilation. Her face was as beautiful as when I had first met her. I looked back at the blur of scenery. I knew then that I was leading her through time to the person she was in the 1950s. As I looked back at her, she was changing into Bobbie-Lou. She pulled me close to her and kissed me. The kiss was as sweet as I had dreamed before. Soft and warming.

I awoke to nuzzle from Moonbeam. Boo was already up, smoking a Chesterfield and sitting on Moonbeam.

"What time is it?" I asked.

"How the hell should I know?" Boo grunted. "My watch says it's one thirty, but then it was one twenty when we started our nap. Must be time to go. Moonbeam is chompin' at the bit."

I grabbed my BB gun/rifle, strapped on my satchel, and joined Boo on Moonbeam. We trotted off to the west toward Camp Douglas.

We got to the top of the hill behind the outhouses and dismounted. Moonbeam walked back down the hill and lost herself in the shadows.

"Which crapper do you think he'll use?" Boo asked.

"The one we don't lock," I said. We walked cautiously toward the two outhouses. Boo was unraveling the string as I sneaked around to the front of the outhouses. I opened the door to the one on my right. It smelled bad enough to blow up without carbide tablets. The latching mechanism was just a piece of wood with a nail through one end, holding it loosely to the wall. On the door was a slot the other piece of wood dropped into from the top. I propped up the piece of latch so that it was almost straight up, but leaned a little toward the door. I then carefully closed the door and gave a sharp rap to the wall side of the door. I heard the wood latch plop into place. I pulled on the door to make sure it was tightly locked. It was. I opened the second outhouse door and dumped all of the carbide pellets through the open hole. I heard a sizzle as the carbide absorbed moisture from the existing, reeking pile of shit. All of the gas would not escape. It would take a lot more than moist feces to make it change into acetylene.

When I got back to the rear of the outhouse, Boo had fastened the string to the top of the outhouse where a moon-shaped vent was located. We played out the string as we silently went to our perch at the top of the hill. I fastened a large chunk of rocket fuel to two paper clips under Boo's watchful eyes. Then we waited.

It was a beautiful morning. The sun was dawning over our shoulders. It must have been a Saturday or Sunday, because there were no formations in the quadrangle, and all but a couple of soldiers were up. High clouds in the east allowed the sun to cast a reddish hue on their undersides. The air was still, and the birds were chirping and singing, greeting the sun. Somewhere a horse, not Moonbeam, whinnied. The air smelled fresh and sweet, but that was soon to change.

Colonel Connor was just waking. Next to him in bed was a whore from town. She was one of the "gate hangers," as the soldiers called them. They were used and abused, and Colonel Connor was no saint in that regard. He looked over at the woman and winced. Her perfume from the night before had worn thin, allowing the natural smell of someone who had not bathed in a week to be noticeable. There was an empty bottle of rye whiskey on the floor beside the cot. The colonel swung his legs over the side of the bed and pulled the suspenders attached to his red flannel long johns over his shoulders.

God, I've got to piss, he thought. Quietly, so as not to wake his snoring partner, he slipped on his boots and headed for the rear door to the HQ building. "I'm glad I don't have to piss and shit in a slit trench," he whispered to himself as he opened the door and looked up at the beautiful sky, his last. He half limped toward the outhouse; his overfull bladder causing pain in his groin.

"Shit, damn, hell," he said as he tried the outhouse door on his left. "Damn thing is locked," he mumbled. Without hesitating he grabbed for the other door, opened it, and stumbled in. He sat down and immediately drained his bladder into the open hole. His bowels also let loose, and vacated his colon with a loud noise. Several farts followed in a staccato fashion.

"Jesus Christ, that stinks," he said, as the deadly gas bubbled forth from the pellets. He could not hear the sizzle until it was too late. Even then, he would not have guessed what it was.

"Now," I said as we heard his blasphemy. I pulled the string tight and held the fuel while Boo lit it with the tip of his Chesterfield. The rock immediately started to burn. A purple flame shot out as I released it, allowing gravity to pull it toward the vent, which was now spewing forth a cloud of invisible acetylene vapor. The fuel, swinging side to side, left a trail of smoke like a snake slithering toward an unsuspecting rat. When the fuel rock banged against the side of the outhouse, Boo and I ducked behind the hill. We knew what would happen next. We first heard the colonel ask, "What the hell is that?" Then we heard a loud whoosh as the first of the vapors ignited. Then a loud explosion rocked the silence of the morning, sending birds flying and horses panicking. All the horses, that is, except Moonbeam, who was right behind us ready to whisk us away to the future.

What we didn't see was the outhouse roof flying fifty feet up and three hundred feet west, landing in the middle of the quadrangle. The colonel soon followed, but not in one piece. The walls of the outhouse were flattened, and shit was everywhere. Even the adjoining outhouse was leveled. As Moonbeam sped us away, Boo and I started laughing, all the way back to the future. I swear I even heard Moonbeam laugh, if horses can laugh.

When we got back to the fort, to our surprise, Teak-qua was there. He must have stoked the fire, because it was burning brightly. As we scooted around the fire, Teak-qua stopped his chanting and looked at us.

"What are you doing up?" Boo asked. "You were always gone when we got back before."

"I wanted to thank you for the clever way you took care of the colonel," he said. "He got what he deserved."

"He didn't suffer enough," I responded. "Not for what he did to Nightstar.

"He suffered," Teak-qua said. "If you stayed around long enough, you would have noticed that he was not killed instantly. He landed in one place, and his manhood, separated by the explosion, landed beside him. He was able to reach out and pick up his manhood, it was so close. It took him a few seconds to realize they were his. When he did, he howled, not only from the realization, but also from the incredible pain. He lived another fifteen minutes in agony before bleeding to death. No one would help him because he was covered from head to toe in feces. No one even touched him when they buried him. They tied a rope to his leg and dragged him with a horse to the field. He was pushed into a grave, and his privates thrown in on top of him. They did not even put him in a wooden box."

"That's more than the Shoshone received," I said. "At least he suffered some."

"Teak-qua," Boo said. "Are you able to appear in the daytime?"

"If I need to," he said. "I can appear anytime. Why do you ask?" I looked at Boo with the expression on my face of *yeah, why did you ask?*

"I thought you might want to go with us to the movies this afternoon," Boo explained. It might be something to do rather than stay in the cave all day."

Are you out of your mind? I thought. *How do we explain him to the girls?*

"What is a movie?" Teak-qua asked, showing interest.

"You go to a theater, in a building, and watch pictures that move," Boo explained. "It's like you are dreaming wide awake. You get to see all kinds of action."

"We're taking the girls," I reminded Boo.

"He can follow us there from Cherry Avenue, and go in after we do," Boo said. "You can't bring the pipe, but you can smoke cigarettes. You can sit in the back row, and nobody will notice you."

"Dressed like this, he'll draw a lot of attention," I said.

"He's my dad's size," Boo continued. "I can bring him shoes, pants, and a shirt. He can put them on, go through the woods, and meet us on Cherry. Teak-qua, you can follow at a safe distance. We'll buy your ticket and hand it to you. Follow us into the theater and we'll point to where you can sit. We'll go past the last rows and sit in the middle. Tie your hair back too, and tuck it under the shirt. I'll leave my watch with my dad's clothes. You can meet us on Cherry between one and one fifteen."

"Sounds like a good plan to me," I said. "What do you think, Teak-qua. Ya wanna go?"

"Let me sleep on it," Teak-qua responded. "Get the clothes and put them here on the table. If I can get them on and decide to go, I will meet you on the place you call Cherry."

"Let's show you tonight how to get there," I said.

"That is good," Teak-qua said.

Boo and I scooted out of the cave, followed by Teak-qua. Using the flashlight, we crept through the woods and came out on Cherry Avenue, where there was a vacant lot designated for an alleyway. Across Cherry was Twenty-Third Street, where the alleyway would become an extension. The lot remains vacant today. When we got back to the fort, Teak-qua assured us he could find his way. Boo showed him that one o'clock was when Roy's pistol hand was pointing at the one and his other hand was pointing straight up. We crawled in our bags, as Teak-qua sat cross-legged in the back of the fort, chanting and smoking.

Eight

I woke up to the sound of Boo pulling on a cigarette.

"Morning, glory," Boo said. I heard my dad use that term, which is where, I suspect, Boo learned it when we were smaller and used to sleep over at each other's homes.

"Morning," I said. "Give me a cigarette. I'm out." He handed me a cigarette. I looked toward the back of the fort and saw Teak-qua's bones were back in their place. "Today's the day we take the girls to the movies. I still have to cut my dad's grass too," I continued, lighting the cigarette from Boo's lit one.

"Yeah," Boo countered. "I have to cut ours too. I guess we better get started. Meet me at my house about one o'clock. The movie starts at one thirty. We'll walk over to Bobbie-Lou's and pick her up. Linda will most likely be there too. I think those two are never apart. I hope Teak-qua makes it." Boo got up and left. I had forgotten we invited Teak-qua. I finished my cigarette and headed for home.

After I cut our grass, I washed up. We only took a bath on Saturday night. I didn't know people bathed daily until I went in the navy. I got as clean as I could by washing my face, hands, and arms.

I put on a clean pair of Levis and a clean T-shirt. I only had one pair of sneakers (tennis shoes were called sneakers then) and checked my pocket to make sure I had enough money. I had $2.50, so I did not need to make a trip to my sister's piggy bank. I could feel among the change the pendant given to me by Hunts Bear, and taken from the hand of Nightstar.

"Where are you going?" my mom asked, as I walked through the kitchen and out the back door.

"Boo and I are going to the movies," I responded, pausing long enough to see that she was making gnocchi for tonight's dinner.

Gnocchi's are similar to potato dumplings. They were my dad's favorite Italian dish. They were good, but they made you thirsty. When you drank anything to quench the thirst, the gnocchi swelled up and distended your stomach. As kids, we learned not to eat so many, but unsuspecting guests did not fare so well. When my sister brought home her fiancé years later, to taste my mother's homemade Italian fare, the rest of us watched him pack away way too many gnocchi. We never thought to warn him, as he kept proclaiming how good they were, at the same time heaping more on his plate. Nothing makes an Italian mother happier than a person with a healthy appetite. He was a big, strong man with a healthy appetite. My mother was pleased.

After dinner, I went with my sister and her fiancé to the church auditorium to play volleyball. After the first set, the fiancé headed to the water cooler. I looked at my sister and smiled. She did not say anything to him. After all, he was an adult. By the fifth set, and after many trips to the water fountain, the fiancé was in obvious pain. For one thing, he couldn't jump anymore and was slowed down by his swelling gut. By the end of the game, he was lying on the floor moaning, his stomach the size of the volleyball. As we helped him to the car, we explained the art of just eating a few gnocchi, so as not to suffer later. He was okay the next day, but a lot wiser.

"What movie?" my mother inquired.

"Mount Union Theater," I called back, heading out the door and onto the back porch. I knew she wanted the name of the movie, but I did not want to discuss the matter any further. This was my first date, and I was nervous. Explaining things to my mother was not what I wanted to do. If she said anything else as I headed down the driveway toward Boo's house, I did not hear it.

"Hey, Boo, I'm here," I shouted in through his kitchen screen door.

"Comin'," Boo said. His mother was in the basement, so he did not get the third degree as I had.

"Did you get the clothes for Teak-qua?" I asked.

"Yeah," Boo said. "I put them in the fort around eleven thirty. I went the back way, up past the old lady's house and through the back woods. She musta been eatin' lunch, so I ducked through her yard. I didn't want to be seen carrying clothes, so I put them in a grocery sack."

The old lady and her husband lived next to our house, across the vacant lot that also was to be the other end of the Twenty-Third Street extension. They were first-generation Hungarians and the oldest people on the street. All of their children were grown up and lived in other cities. The old lady sat all day on her small front porch and watched everything that happened on Watson Avenue. She was a large woman, with her hair pulled back in a bun. She looked like the mother of the Katzenjammer Kids in the Sunday funnies, but unlike the sometimes-smiling "Mamma," she had a constant scowl on her face. My sisters and I were not their favorite people, ever since the incident.

I don't know what game we were playing, but it required us to say "hunky dory" a lot. The old lady thought we were calling her a hunky, slang for Hungarian. Until that incident, we didn't even know they were Hungarian. When her husband got home from work, we heard her hollering at him in a foreign language. Unlike the rather large and bearded "Der Captain" of the Katzenjammers, he was rather short and puny, and constantly browbeaten by his much larger and boisterous wife. During the old lady's tirade, I was playing in the driveway in the vacant lot. The next thing I knew, Der Captain, had me by the back of my shirt and hauled me to my back door. He told my mother we were calling him names. I had no idea what he was talking about. My mother did not like the way he was manhandling me and she let him know it. From then on we were like the Hatfields and McCoys.

Der Captain had a garden on the hill behind his house. Adjacent to the garden was a small shed, where he kept his equipment and a table for drying peppers. Boo and I decided one day to get even for the hunky incident and, from the safety of the Watson Woods, shot out the windows in his shed with our BB guns. I don't know how he did it on his own, but the next Saturday, the shed was relocated down the hill and attached to the garage. It is still there to this day.

Since we couldn't shoot out the windows anymore, we decided to direct our mischief toward the old lady. Boo had a signal mirror that had a see-through X cut in the middle for aiming. On the backside of the mirror was another smaller mirror surrounding the X. The trick was to look through the X in the mirror and align the X-shaped reflection the sun made on your shoulder with the see-through X. When the Xs were aligned, the sun's reflection on the front of the mirror was precisely aimed at whatever was in the center of the see-through X. One very sunny day, from Boo's front yard, five houses away, we aimed the Xs at the old lady's perch on her front porch.

Within seconds, she ducked through the front door and into her house. We waited for a few minutes, and sure enough, she came back out. We nailed her again. She tried to shield the glare with her hands, but we were persistent. We drove her back in her house again. We were convinced we could do this indefinitely. Because of the sun's glare, she could not see where the light was coming from. This was our fun for that day. We played the same game all that summer whenever the conditions were right, but she won out when we grew tired of the game.

Der Captain's shed was not my first episode breaking windows. When I was in first grade, I thought it would be fun to break out all the windows in one of the grade school teacher's garage. One of my classmates saw me, saving one of the windows. He told the teacher and I was confronted the next day after school. On my way home, my dad picked me up in his car. He came after me because I was late getting home. I had a reputation for stopping and petting the neighbor's dogs, one time causing me to be miss lunch.

"Where have you been?" he asked, when he found me.

"I had to stay late and tell on a boy who broke some windows," I said, my first really big lie of a growing career.

Of course, the teacher called that night with the truth. That same evening, using a nearby streetlight to see, my dad replaced all the broken windows. When he got home, he was too tired to mete out punishment, which probably saved my life.

"Let's go pick up the girls," Boo said. We headed down the driveway and crossed the street to Bobbie-Lou's house. My stomach felt funny as Boo knocked on the door. Bobbie-Lou's mother appeared. She was a beautiful woman, the most attractive one in the neighborhood. She was shapely, with a thin waist, large breasts, and a rounded butt. Boo and I could not help but stare with our mouths agape.

"Is Bobbie-Lou here?" Boo finally asked, breaking out of his trance.

"I understand you're going to the movies with her and Linda," she said, smiling. "That's very nice of you." I thought she winked at us, but from behind the screen door, it was hard to tell.

"I'll go get the girls." This confirmed what we thought earlier, that Linda was there too.

Boo and I waited in silence until Bobbie-Lou and Linda opened the door.

"Hi," Bobbie-Lou said. I felt my heart melt. She looked great. She had on a light blue sack dress, stylish for that time. Her hair was long and shiny, with a bejeweled bobby pin holding the left side close to her head. The dress was short, almost too short, but I wasn't going to complain. I noticed the bumps where her breasts were starting to form. Even though the sack dress hung straight down, it bulged outward in the back. Bobbie-Lou was going to have her mother's shape when she fully matured.

Linda also was wearing a sack dress, only hers did not hang on her as nicely as Bobbie-Lou's. Devoid of any shape whatsoever, Linda's dress hung straight down. It was longer too, reaching below the knees. It was a good thing too, because Linda's knees were knobby and wrinkled. Bobbie-Lou's were smooth, with almost no bumps except where a scab had formed from the "accident." Linda had on her large, tortoise shell glasses. Her hair was curly but, although blonde, did not look as good as Bobbie-Lou's. Linda would grow up a homely looking person.

"We're going now," Bobbie-Lou called out to her mother.

"Okay," she responded. "You kids have fun."

"Let's go up Catherine Lane and then down Cherry," I suggested. In addition to picking up Teak-qua, I did not want to walk past my house and all the adjacent neighbors' houses. The less my parents, and especially my sisters, found out about my "date," the better. Sisters had a way of teasing that got to me. The last thing I wanted was a rendition of "Andy and Bobbie sitting in a tree, k-i-s-s-i-n-g."

"Okay," Bobbie-Lou said.

"Why?" Linda asked. I ignored her question and led the procession to the right at the end of Bobbie-Lou's driveway.

"Boo and I decided we would pay for the tickets," I said, trying to change the subject.

"Why?" Linda asked. "We can pay our own way."

"You guys buy the popcorn," Boo said.

"Okay," Bobbie-Lou responded. That was enough said on that subject. "What do you guys do every night in that cave?"

"We don't spend every night there," I said. "When it rains, we stay at home. You might not believe this, but there is an Indian that visits us the nights we stay at the fort."

This brought a howl from Linda, but Bobbie-Lou was silent.

"Fort, Indian," Linda said. "You two have been watching too many Western movies. Tell us more about this imaginary friend, Tonto."

"Like I said," I continued. "His name is Teak-qua. Tonto, means stupid in Italian, just like your comment." Score one for the "umbday oybays." "He visits us at night, talks to us, and smokes our cigarettes in a pipe. Those are his bones you saw in the back of the cave. He has a horse named Moonbeam that takes us back in time to avenge the Indians."

Now Bobbie-Lou was looking at me like I had a big booger hanging out.

"You don't have to believe us," I continued. "We invited him to go to the movies with us. We'll point him out if you promise not to make fun of him." We were rounding the corner from Catherine Lane onto Cherry. I looked ahead but did not see Teak-qua.

"What do you do to avenge the Indians?" Bobbie-Lou asked.

"So far we've blown up bad guys." Boo said.

"Eallyray upidstay," Linda said. "Please tell us more lies."

"You don't believe us," I said. "We're not going to say anything else about it."

"If it's true," Bobbie-Lou said. "Can we go with you next time?"

"Teak-qua wakes us up when it's time to go," Boo said. "It's usually around midnight. You would have to sleep in the fort with us if you want to go."

"We could wake you up on our way to get Moonbeam next time," I added. "That is, if Teak-qua says it's okay. I think Moonbeam can carry three of us. She is a big horse, and moves very smoothly. We change a little when we go back in time too."

"How do you change?" Linda asked. "You certainly don't get any smarter."

"We get bigger," Boo responded. "But we always return to our size when we come back to the present. We can speak Indian too."

We passed the vacant Twenty-Third Street lot, but I didn't see any sign of Teak-qua. Maybe he wouldn't show, now that we bragged about him.

"Our BB guns turn into real rifles too," I added.

"Ootay uchmay," Linda said. "I don't know if it's safe to go to the movies with you two liars. Where is Tonto?" Linda and Boo took the lead as Bobbie-Lou and I dropped a couple of paces behind. I was positioned on the street side as I was taught to do when walking with a girl.

"I don't know," Boo said. "He said he may or may not come."

When we got to the corner of Cherry and Mill, the next block toward the theater, I turned around. I saw Teak-qua following behind us by about half a block. Bobbie-Lou turned around and saw him too.

"Is that him?" she whispered to me.

"Yes," I whispered back.

"Why are you two whispering?" Linda asked. She turned around to look at us but did not notice Teak-qua.

"I wanted to see how good those big ears of yours are," I said.

"That's not nice, Andy," Bobbie-Lou said.

"I'm sorry," I said. The last thing I wanted to do was have Linda mad and walk away. Bobbie-Lou was most certainly to go with her.

"We just noticed Teak-qua behind us," I continued. Linda and Boo both turned when I said that.

"Turn back around," I continued. "You might scare him off."

"Andy!" Bobbie-Lou cautioned.

"I didn't mean with your looks," I said. "I meant that he might not like it if we watch him."

"He don't look like no Indian to me," Linda said. "Where's his feathers and that horse of his?"

"He's wearing my dad's clothes," Boo explained. "And we ride Moonbeam, not him." We were approaching State Street, probably the busiest street in the city. I didn't think about the danger of Teak-qua trying to cross.

"Maybe I better go back and help him cross the street," I said. "He might not—"

"No," Boo interrupted. "He can make it on his own. Besides, it's not that busy right now."

"What about your clothes when you get bigger?" Bobbie-Lou asked. "If I go with you and get bigger, my clothes won't fit." She was obviously curious now that she saw Teak-qua. I thought it would be exciting if she came with us. I was also thinking how she would have to hold onto me as we rode bareback.

"They grow with us," I answered. "Your clothes would probably do the same. If you want, you can wear one of your mom's jackets so it will fit you." I really wanted her to go. I was hoping Teak-qua would say yes. She doesn't have to go when we killed someone, just on one of our preview trips.

We were now in sight of the theater. There was no line to get tickets. Boo and Linda were now twenty feet ahead of us, and Boo was approaching the ticket booth. I turned back to see if Teak-qua made it across State Street. He had and was catching up to us.

"I need to buy Teak-qua's ticket," I told Bobbie-Lou. "Wait by the usher for me.

"Two children and one adult," I told the ticket seller.

"That'll be a dollar twenty-five," the elderly lady said. I handed her two bucks and she gave me three quarters back. By that time Teak-qua was approaching the theater.

"Teak-qua," I said, walking to where he was standing. "Here is your ticket. Follow us through the turnstile. The man will take the ticket and tear it in half. Keep the half and meet us inside." Teak-qua said nothing as he stared all around at the brightly colored posters of what movie was showing now and the coming attractions. He gave a little shiver as a blast of air hit him. There was a deep rumble of equipment accompanying the blast of cold air coming from the open doors, right under the sign proclaiming "Air Conditioned Theater."

"It's okay, Teak-qua," I said. "It's just cool air. You'll be fine with the clothes you have on. You'll get used to it."

I walked through the turnstile with Bobbie-Lou in front of me. I handed the man our tickets and turned to see where Teak-qua was. He was approaching the turnstile with confidence. If I were in his shoes, or should I say Boo's dad's shoes, I would have been scared to death.

"Let's get seated first, so I can show Teak-qua where to sit," I said. The smell of popcorn and melting butter permeated the entire lobby. We walked into the dimly lit theater entrance on the right side. I figured there would not be as many people on that side. I did not need to worry, as there were very few people inside. Boo, Linda, and Bobbie-Lou walked halfway down and picked a row. They scooted in while I waited for Teak-qua to come down the aisle. I led him into the next to last row on the side against the wall.

"Do you need any cigarettes," I asked. He shook his head no. "If you need anything, we'll be right down there." I pointed to where Bobbie-Lou and Linda were turned around looking at us. I then joined them as Boo walked back to the lobby.

"Boo went to get the popcorn," Bobbie-Lou said. "We gave him some money. We gave him enough for Teak-qua too."

"Okay," I said. "I hope he'll be all right." They knew I was referring to our Indian friend.

"Can we meet him afterwards?" Linda said. "I'm sorry about the Tonto comments."

"I'll ask him on the way back," I said. "I didn't tell him you knew about him, but from the staring, I think he knows."

The lights started dimming as I turned around to see where Boo was and to check on Teak-qua. Boo was handing Teak-qua a box of popcorn. He made it back to our seats just as the screen played the first rendition of "Let's go out to the lobby," which was the theater's advertisement to encourage patrons to purchase food. He handed me one box of popcorn. I assumed Bobbie-Lou and I would share it. Soon after the second rendition, the cartoon started. It was a Bugs Bunny and Elmer Fudd, my favorite. I took a look back toward Teak-qua. He was eating his popcorn and staring wide-eyed at the silver screen.

When the feature film started, I did the old stretch-your-arm routine and rested my left arm on the metal back of Bobbie-Lou's theater seat. This is what Boo told me to do. He didn't tell me what to do next, and my arm started to fall asleep after several minutes. Bobbie-Lou must have felt sorry for me, because she reached across and back with her left hand and pulled my arm down on her shoulder. She then smiled at me and leaned back, resting her head against the crook of my elbow. She took the box of popcorn, opened it, and held it in her left hand against our armrest. She then draped her right arm over our armrest and placed her hand on my knee.

"That should be more comfortable for both of us," she whispered to me. I felt as if Nightstar had crawled in bed with me again. I was in heaven. We watched the movie and ate the popcorn. Several times, I checked to see if Teak-qua was still there. He was.

When the credits started to roll, the lights came back on. I turned around to see how Teak-qua was doing. I caught a glimpse of him leaving the theater.

"Teak-qua just left," I said. "I hope he can find his way back to the fort."

"I think he'll be all right," Boo said. "Ready to go?"

"Yes," Linda said. "Thanks, boys, I really enjoyed the movie."

"So did I," Bobbie-Lou said. "Let's go back to my house and get some Cokes. I'm thirsty after that popcorn. They always make it too salty."

"That's to make you buy their Cokes here," I said. "They always water them down, and they taste flat too. We could go over to L&J's drugstore and get some cherry Cokes, after we make sure Teak-qua gets back."

"Some other time," Bobbie-Lou said. "Besides, you already paid for the movie. My mom said it would be okay if we sat out on the back porch."

"Okay," I said.

When we left the theater, the afternoon heat hit us after spending two hours in the air-conditioned theater. We could see Teak-qua ahead of us. We talked about the movie on the walk back. Linda said how cute Sidney looked. Bobbie-Lou agreed, but not as enthusiastically. When we got to Cherry Avenue, Teak-qua disappeared into the vacant lot. I deliberately slowed the pace so that Boo and Linda would get out of earshot.

"I have something I'd like to give you, Bobbie-Lou," I said. She looked at me as I reached into my pocket and pulled out the turquoise stone.

I handed it to her, and she looked at it, her mouth agape.

"What's this for?" she asked. "Where did you get it?"

"It was given to me by the Indians for shooting a bear," I said. "Boo got one too. I want you to have it. I don't think I can wear it."

"It's beautiful," she said, turning it over in her hands. "It looks like there is a face in it." She held it up to me, and I thought I could see the image of Nightstar reflected in it. I had not noticed it before. She pulled on my arm and kissed me on the cheek. I immediately felt my face flush, and a tingling up and down my spinal cord.

"Here, help me put it on," she begged. She turned away from me and held the two ends of the rawhide over her shoulders. When I grabbed the two ends, she lifted her hair, and I joined the two ends with a square knot, just like I was taught in Cub Scouts.

When she turned back around she was smiling, and kissed me again on the cheek. Boo and Linda had turned around to see what had happened to us and caught the second kiss. I must have looked like a beet, but felt really good inside.

"What are you two doing?" Linda asked. They stopped to wait for us to catch up.

"Look what Andy gave me," Bobbie-Lou declared. She held up the amulet for Linda to see. "Isn't it beautiful?"

Linda grabbed it and held up to her myopic eyes. She squinted hard at the stone. Boo looked at me with an *Are you nuts?* look in his eyes.

"It looks like plastic to me," Linda declared, hoping it was.

"It's real," Boo blurted out. "I got one just like it, only I'm keeping mine." He pulled his pendant out of his pocket and dangled it in front of Linda. Linda let out a "humph," and we resumed our trek back to Bobbie-Lou's house. Bobbie-Lou had a smile on her face the whole way back. She held the stone with her left hand. She reached down and held my left hand in her right. I thought, *This is it, I'm really in love.*

When we got to Bobbie-Lou's, we sat on chairs on the backyard patio. Her mother brought us ice-cold Cokes and some homemade cookies. She sat with us as we told her about the movie. Bobbie-Lou had tucked the stone under her dress, so her mother never saw it. I was glad, because I couldn't think of a lie about where I got it. Teak-qua was not mentioned to her mother.

At four thirty, Bobbie-Lou's dad got home. Recalling his promise to cut my ears off, I said I had to get home for supper. Boo said he had to go too, so we both left at the same time.

"Are you going to play kickball tonight?" Bobbie-Lou asked.

"Yeah, sure," I said. "See ya." Cut-Your-Ears-Off was giving me a dirty look as I headed toward my house. Before going home, I took a look in the fort to see if Teak-qua made it okay. His bones were in place in the back wall, and Boo's dad's clothes were neatly stacked on the table.

After our game of kickball, Bobbie-Lou and I sat on the curb together. Boo and Linda sat on the curb on the opposite side of the street. I was tossing Mugsy's rock, and he was retrieving it tirelessly.

"Are you going to travel back in time tonight?" Bobbie-Lou asked. "If so, I would really like to go."

"I don't know," I said. "Teak-qua always wakes us up on the nights we are to travel. We never know when."

"If it's tonight, come get me," she said.

"We'll have to ask Teak-qua if it's okay first," I said. "What about your father? He really doesn't like me after the bike accident. If he catches me around your house, he'll kill me."

"He sleeps soundly," she said. "I'll leave my window open, and you can wake me, please."

"Okay," I said. "Mugsy won't bark will he?"

"Mugsy sleeps in my room, but he never barks," she said.

It was getting dark, and Linda's mother was calling her to come home. As I was getting ready to stand up, Bobbie-Lou tugged at my arm and planted a kiss on my cheek. When she turned her face forward, I returned the kiss. She had a sparkle in her eyes as she grabbed the turquoise stone and held it close to her heart. We both stood up as Boo came across the street toward us. Bobbie-Lou headed home with Mugsy close behind. She had on her tightest short shorts, and I stared at her until she closed the front door behind her.

"You got it bad," Boo said. We then headed for the fort.

Nine

We awoke that night as usual to Teak-qua's chanting. After we both lit up, we got Teak-qua's attention and asked him how he liked the movies.

"It was like I was dreaming," he said. "There was another world I was taken to. Thank you for including me. I especially enjoyed the buffalo soldier."

"Buffalo soldier?" Boo asked.

"He means Sidney Poitier," I said. "Negroes were called that when they fought the Indians. They got the name from their hair. It was like a buffalo's, so the Indians called them buffalo soldiers."

"Did you like the popcorn," Boo asked.

"Yes, but I had to drink a lot of water from the stream below the fort on my way back."

"You drank from a sewer?" I said. "You're lucky you are still alive."

"My life ended many years ago," he said. "You have done well on your trips, my warriors," Teak-qua said. "There is a lot more

163

that needs to be done to avenge my people, but I am afraid it will never be accomplished."

"We found out that some of the warriors from the Shoshone's killed some settlers," I said. "This was before the soldiers came and destroyed them and their village,"

"Yes," Teak-qua continued. "There was wrong on both sides back then, but the white man's punishment of my people did not stop with the massacres you have witnessed. The white man invaded our lands; we fought back when we could, but we were outnumbered. We were forced to give up our best lands; forced to live on reservations; forced to go to the white man's school; forced to accept the white man's religion, food, and way of life. We had treaties, which were broken, and still today are being broken. Did you know that the United States had promised to take care of our education, housing, and health until the rivers run dry and mountains are washed to the sea? Yet today, many of my people live in poverty, ignorance, and poor health because of the broken promises of the white man. Yes, we did some killing of our own, but lost our souls in the process."

"Where do we go tonight?" Boo asked.

"The place you call Colorado Territory," Teak-qua responded. "You will visit my friend Black Kettle, chief of a small band of Cheyenne and Arapaho. A three-year-old treaty is about to be broken by soldiers in command of Colonel John Chivington. That is all I am going to tell you. Now go. Moonbeam awaits at the place called country club."

"Teak-qua," I said. "Bobbie-Lou wants to go with us. Is this possible? I mean, she won't say anything."

"She is the one I saw you with at the dream place, is she not?"

"Yes, she is a friend of mine and won't be any trouble, I promise."

"Then take her along," he said. "Moonbeam will make sure she is safe."

"Thanks," I said. "It means a lot to me."

We grabbed our guns and knapsacks and headed for another adventure.

"I sure hope this one isn't as bad as the last," I told Boo. "I don't think I could watch another brutal show like that."

"Me either," Boo said. "I don't think it's a good idea to bring Bobbie-Lou along. Linda asked too, but I told her no way. I ain't as attached to her as you are to Bobbie-Lou. You've got it real bad for her. Hopefully, she won't have to see us kill someone."

"Well, let's stop by and get her. She said she would leave her window open. She's in the back bedroom." We took the back way to Bobbie-Lou's house. There was a trail in the woods that ran down the hill behind all the houses on the west side of Watson. The woods started fifty feet from the top of the hill. The trail was where we hid when we shot out the windows in Mr. Holtzer's shed. Most lots had fences at the end of the property line at the start of the woods, but Bobbie-Lou's did not.

"I hope her old man is a sound sleeper," Boo said. "If he wakes up, you'll look funny with no ears." When we got to the point behind Bobbie-Lou's house, we crouched low and moved across the open field at the top of the hill. Using the detached garage as a shield, we dropped down the bank and slid along the house side of the garage.

"Wait here," I whispered. "I'll go get her."

I did almost a duck walk to get to the bedroom window. When I stood up, I saw that she did have her window up. Cut-Your-Ears-Off was in the room next to this one, but the two windows for that bedroom were closed.

"Bobbie-Lou," I whispered, as loud as I dared. There was no response.

"Bobbie-Lou," I said again, a little louder. I ran my fingernail over the window screen, hoping to add a little more noise different from my voice. There was no response. I gave up and sat down outside the window, wondering whether to give up or try again.

"Andy, is that you?" Bobbie-Lou whispered. She was at the window and looking out.

"Yes," I said and stood up. "Teak-qua is sending us on another trip tonight. Do you still want to go?"

"Yes. I'll be out in a minute."

"We'll wait behind the garage."

"Wait, help me out of the window," she said. I heard the muffled sound of her putting on clothes. I was hoping she did not wear the tight, short shorts. I didn't know what would happen to them when she got bigger.

She was dressed and working at the screen, when the light went on in the hallway outside her open bedroom door. She ducked down, and I did too. My heart was racing as I heard footsteps coming down the hall. I started praying under my breath ... *now and at the hour of our death.* I heard a toilet flush, and the footsteps retreated down the hall. I let out the breath I had been holding for the last minute. Bobbie-Lou started working at the screen to take it out of the frame.

She handed me the screen when she had it free from its four retaining rings. I put it on the ground, leaning against the house.

"Cup your hands and give me a step," she whispered. I made a step by interlacing my fingers in the same manner Boo and I got on Moonbeam. She stuck her left leg out the window and put her foot in my hands. She was wearing jeans and red sneakers. I never noticed before how tiny her feet were. She swung the rest of her body out of the window, twisting so that she was facing me, her hands resting on my shoulders. I lowered her to the ground and she stepped out of my hands. She had a white, long-sleeved blouse tied at the middle, open at the top. Under that was a tight-fitting, red T-shirt. She smiled at me and grabbed my hand. In her other hand she held a small, black leather bag. With our heads ducked, we headed for Boo, who was hiding behind the garage.

"Hi, Boo," she said.

"Man, I thought you two were goners when I saw the light come on the hallway," Boo said. "That's when I made for the back of the garage." He grabbed my right ear, and then the left. "Yep, still attached." Bobbie-Lou laughed.

"Where are we going?" she asked.

"Moonbeam is at the country club," I responded. "Let's go."

The country club was where the rich people in town went. We did too in the winter, for sledding and skiing. There also was a pond for ice skating. The other seasons, the country club was a golf course, where occasionally, on a rainy day, we found a few lost golf balls. It was also a good place to pick up a few dollars as a caddy, but Boo and I never did. Of course, the entrepreneur David did as soon as he was old enough. Parts of the course ran adjacent to Silver Park, separated by a barbed-wire fence. The main entrance was off of Milton Street, which, to avoid Mr. Kidwell, was where we headed.

Bobbie-Lou and I did not hold hands on the way to the club, but she did walk beside me and occasionally we bumped into each other. I was feeling really happy by the time we got there.

"Where's Moonbeam?" Bobbie-Lou asked.

"I think I see her over there, standing beside the park fence," Boo said. "We always find her." This last comment was for Bobbie-Lou.

When we approached, Moonbeam came out of the tree shadows cast by the moon. Bobbie-Lou's eyes lit up at the sight of such a beautiful animal.

"Hi, Moonbeam," I said. She whinnied then trotted over to nudge me on the chest. She nudged Boo too, and then took a long, almost jealous look at Bobbie-Lou.

"This is Bobbie-Lou," I explained. "Teak-qua said she could go with us." Moonbeam shook her head up and down, as if giving her approval too.

"What do we do now?" Bobbie-Lou asked.

"We get on her and ride, upidstay irlgay," Boo said.

"Come on, Boo," I said. "Bobbie-Lou doesn't know."

"Oh, I forgot, you two are in love," Boo said. Moonbeam bumped him a little harder than before, knocking him back a step.

"Let's go," Bobbie-Lou said. "Help me up."

"I'll get on first," I said. "Then Boo will make a step for you, while I pull you up."

Bobbie-Lou swung up behind me, and we both reached down and pulled Boo up behind Bobbie-Lou.

"Giddyup," Boo said. Moonbeam started her usual trot.

Bobbie-Lou, feeling the first movement, let out a little squeak and put both arms around my waist, resting her cheek against my back. Her arms felt warm and gentle, her breath hot against my skin. Boo and I held our BB guns loosely across Moonbeam's back with both hands as we usually did. I was not about to tell Bobbie-Lou she did not have to hang on. As we rose higher, I felt her release her grip a bit, and her face came off my back. She was looking around in amazement.

When Moonbeam straightened out and started to speed up, I said very coolly, "This is where the fun begins."

As the stars started to streak by and the moon became a slivery blur, Bobbie-Lou said the only thing I heard during the trip.

"Oh my God, this is fantastic," she said, in wonderment. I could feel her turning her head from side to side. To my satisfaction, she kept her arms around my waist.

We arrived, this time at mid-morning, judging by the height of the sun. It was warm, but it did not feel like the heat of a beginning summer day. The sky was the bluest I had ever seen. There must have been no humidity to stop the bright rays of the sun from kissing the earth.

Moonbeam descended to a flat, prairie landscape next to a wide creek. Far away to the west, there were towering mountains. The prairie-like landscape stretched as far as we could see in all other directions. When we approached the ground, Bobbie-Lou tightened her grip on my waist. She only relaxed when Moonbeam trotted to a stop on the grass-covered soil. Boo hopped down, unaided.

"Need some help?" he said to Bobbie-Lou. His voice had deepened from growing older, something I hadn't noticed on previous trips.

"No, I'm fine," was Bobbie-Lou's response. Her voice had somehow changed too. She slid off of Moonbeam, and I did the same. When I turned to her, I could not help but blurt out what I saw.

"Wow, you're beautiful," I said. I was embarrassed as soon as I said it, and she blushed. Bobbie-Lou's transformation was much greater than Boo's or mine. Her face looked more like Nightstar than when we left Ohio. However, her jeans and tied-back shirt accented her body more than Nightstar's Indian dress. When she got over my embarrassing comment, she looked at me with similar amazement. She looked at Boo too and then back at me. She took a mirror out of her bag and looked at herself.

"Is this permanent?" she asked. Her voice was sort of skeptical, as if she wanted the change to stay.

"No," Boo said. "We turn back into pumpkins at midnight."

"No," I said to reassure her. "Boo and I have done this five times so far, and we change back on the return trip."

"Will we get back before my dad gets up?" she asked.

"On the previous trips, we got back before three o'clock, no matter how long it seemed we stayed in the past," Boo said. He looked at his wrist, but Roy was not there. "Dang. Teak-qua didn't give me back my watch. It wasn't with my dad's clothes, or if it was, it's in the wash, where I tossed the clothes. If my mom finds it in my dad's pants or shirt pocket, that would be funny."

"Maybe it's still at the fort," I suggested.

"I'll look for it when we get back," he said.

"It was one o'clock when you woke me," Bobbie-Lou said. "Where are we?"

"Teak-qua said we would go to Colorado Territory," I said. "So we must be in Colorado."

"It must be before 1876, when Colorado became a state," she said. I was amazed at how smart she was. I knew she was good at school, and her knowing when Colorado became a state reinforced that.

"Teak-qua said we would meet Black Kettle, a Cheyenne and Arapaho chief," I said. I looked at her for more information about the Indians, but got none.

"When we were up in the air, I saw an encampment. It was that way, near where this creek was formed by two others," Boo said, pointing toward the north.

"Moonbeam," I said, "lead us to Black Kettle." She shook her head up and down, and we started walking toward where Boo had pointed, following Moonbeam.

"Is she always that smart?" Bobbie-Lou asked.

"She is the smartest horse in the world," I said with pride. We took up positions alongside Moonbeam, Bobbie-Lou and I on her right, Boo on her left.

"Your BB guns look real," she said.

"They are," I responded. "So far, we only used them to shoot a couple of bears."

"I thought Linda wanted to come too," Bobbie-Lou said.

"She did," Boo said. "I don't trust her to keep her mouth shut about the trip. I don't trust you either, but that's Andy's worry."

"I promised not to say anything," she said, "and I always keep my promises."

We told her about the other trips as we walked along, omitting the part about the mutilated bodies we found. We came up over a small rise. About a quarter mile away were the first teepees, too many to count. They covered an area about the size of four or five football fields.

As we got closer, a group of men came out to greet us.

"I am Motovato," the forward most member of the small group said, only the name translated to Black Kettle. He was a short man and wore nothing to make him look like a chief. He was dressed like some of the others, in plain, cloth pants and a long-sleeved, flannel shirt. His eyes were sunken, nose broad, and hair braided in two long, black strands hanging over each shoulder. Some of the men behind him wore colorful shirts; some were naked above the waist.

"I'm Andy, this is Boo, and this is Nightstar, I mean Bobbie-Lou." I said. Bobbie-Lou looked at me with a puzzled look on her face. I held out my hand in greeting after Boo shook Black Kettle's hand. Black Kettle took my hand in a warm double handclasp. He did not shake it, but just held on and gazed into my eyes. It was if he were looking into my soul. He let go of my hand, glanced at Bobbie-Lou, and smiled.

"Follow us to my tent," Black Kettle said. He and the other men turned around and led us toward the tents.

"You spoke their language," Bobbie-Lou whispered. "And I understood it. Can I speak that way too?"

"I assume you can," I answered. "Boo and I always can, and when we talk to each other it comes out in English."

"Who is Nightstar?" she said, in somewhat of a jealous tone.

"An Indian girl we met on a previous trip." I said. "She looked just like you. She died." I lowered my head and held back the tears.

"Oh," was her only response.

We approached a tent in the middle of the camp that had a huge, thirty-four-star American flag hanging from a pole next to it. Doing as the others did, we placed our rifles in a stack at the entrance to the teepee. As we entered the tent, Black Kettle looked surprised when Bobbie-Lou followed us in.

"Teak-qua sent all of us," I said, answering his concern about Bobbie-Lou being in the tent with us. There were no other women present. Reluctantly, he allowed her to stay for whatever was to be said. We all sat down in a circle, cross-legged. Some of the Indians sat behind others, while Boo and I had a front-row seat. Bobbie-Lou sat behind me.

"Teak-qua said you would help us with the white man," Black Kettle said. One of the other braves behind him handed a long-stemmed smoking pipe forward to Black Kettle. He paused long enough to light it and take a long draw. Boo started to reach for a pack of Chesterfields, but I grabbed his arm and with a little shake of my head, indicating he should wait.

"I want nothing but peace," Black Kettle continued. "Some of the young men in the tribes have caused trouble." He handed the pipe to the man on his left.

Hunts Bear had the same problem, I thought, but said nothing.

"We call the troublemakers 'Dog Soldiers.' They have chosen to follow the fighter Roman Nose rather than our peaceful ways. Because of the raids of Roman Nose and the Dog Soldiers, all the Cheyenne and Arapaho have been ordered here to Sand Creek under the protection of Fort Lyon, a half day's hard ride north.

"Lean Bear and I have even been to see Mr. Lincoln," Black Kettle went on, waving his hand in a wide gesture. "His commissioner, Colonel Greenwood, gave us the flag that is hanging outside. He said anyone standing under it would not be harmed. We were given these medals." He pulled out a string of medals hanging on rawhide around his neck. "We were also given papers telling all we are good friends of the United States.

"Lean Bear and I were like brothers. We grew up together, hunted together, and fought together. When we were camped at Ash Creek, Lean Bear was killed riding out to greet the Blue Coats who we thought were on a friendly visit. Lean Bear was waving his medals and our peace papers when he was gunned down. White Antelope and I met with the Blue Coats when they came into camp. No one else was harmed." The man sitting to his left, similarly dressed but with one long braid of hair hanging over his right shoulder, nodded, indicating he was White Antelope. "But now I have heard that soldiers are going to attack our camp. The white soldiers have already made raids on those who stayed on the plains and did not surrender, as we have."

There was a long pause. The pipe had reached me. I took a long pull on it and almost choked. The tobacco was very harsh and strong. I exhaled without inhaling the smoke. Clearly they were waiting on Boo or me to say something. Boo realized this and took the pipe from me, leaving me with nothing to do but speak.

"We can go and talk to the soldiers," I said. "Maybe they will listen to us. If that doesn't work, we will ask for guidance from Teak-qua when we go back."

"You can take our peace papers if you want," Black Kettle said. "When will you go?"

"We should go today, so that if it is necessary, we can go back to talk to Teak-qua tonight," I said. "I don't think taking the papers is necessary. If they shot Lean Bear when he had them, they won't do us any good."

The pipe had completed the circle and was handed back to Black Kettle from the right.

"Then you better get started," Black Kettle said. "It will take you almost all day riding three to a horse." He rose, and so did the rest of us in the tent.

"Moonbeam is a special horse," Boo said. "She will get us there in no time."

With that said, Boo, Bobbie-Lou, and I left the tent, picking up our rifles from the stack.

"This is a change from what we've done in the past," I spoke in English, mostly for Bobbie-Lou's benefit. We were out of Black Kettle's hearing range, the only one I thought could understand us. "Teak-qua never asked us to intervene before. If we can prevent what happened at Bear River, I'll try anything."

"Me too," Boo said.

"What happened at Bear River?" Bobbie-Lou asked.

As we walked to the edge of the camp, where Moonbeam was waiting, Boo and I told Bobbie-Lou all we could about the massacre, not describing the mutilations we saw. The afternoon sun was getting hot, and the air was dusty. I wished we were back at LaNave's swimming pool so we could cool off with a dip in the water. Boo must have been thinking about it too, because he asked about a dip in the creek.

"Let's go skinny-dipping," he said. "That water looks nice and cool."

"Okay," I said. "Bobbie-Lou, you want to tag along?"

"I don't want to skinny-dip," she said, "but I'll wade in the water."

"Chicken," Boo said.

"If I take my clothes off, I'll do it out of view of you two," she said.

"Do what you want," Boo said. Moonbeam spotted us and trotted to where we were.

"Hey, girl," I said, greeting Moonbeam. "Let's ride Moonbeam upstream away from the camp, and then hit the water."

"You're on," Boo said. He hopped on her first. I boosted Bobbie-Lou up behind him, and they both helped me on behind Bobbie-Lou. Moonbeam started off at a trot. Fearing Bobbie-Lou would put her arms around Boo, I put my hands on her waist and told her how to ride without holding on.

"Moonbeam is very gentle," I explained. "Just sit up straight and let your hands rest on your legs, like this." She looked over her shoulder as I reluctantly let go of her waist. She then reached back and took hold of my hands and replaced them on her waist.

"Okay, but hold on to me anyway. It makes me feel better." It made me feel better too.

"You two are making me sick," Boo said. "I'll be glad when we get back."

Bobbie-Lou leaned back against me as Moonbeam trotted off to the north. Her hair was whisking about my face causing a tingling sensation. When we got to a bend in the river, out of sight of the camp, Moonbeam stopped. Boo and I got off.

"Moonbeam," I instructed. "Take Bobbie-Lou further so she can bathe by herself. Please stay by her for protection." Moonbeam shook her head, and, with Bobbie-Lou on her back, proceeded to trot further upstream toward another bend.

Boo and I stripped down to nothing and jumped in the river. We both let out a howl as the chilly water caught us by surprise. The water was only four feet deep, barely up to our chests, but it felt good. We splashed around for awhile, and then lay back against the far bank and stared at the clouds drifting in the bright blue sky.

"Let's sneak up on Bobbie-Lou," Boo said, after a minute. "I never saw a real live naked woman before." We both had seen naked pictures of women in the magazines Boo found under his father's bed. Breasts were the only parts showing in those early girly magazines. Someone did show us a deck of dirty cards one time that they found on the way to school, but we didn't know what we were looking at.

"Okay," I agreed. "But we better not get caught." So we started a slow crawl in the water along the bank of the creek toward the bend where Moonbeam was headed with Bobbie-Lou.

When we rounded the bend, there was Bobbie-Lou, much as we had been earlier, lying against the sand with only her head above the water. Moonbeam was nearby, splashing in the deeper part of the water.

The moving stream was lapping at Bobbie-Lou as we spied on her. We were hoping she would get up so we could see her entire body. I started to daydream, as if I were the stream, flowing around her, licking at her soft skin, cooling her off, and wrapping around her front to back. Then, holding her in a gentle embrace and satisfying her every need and desire.

I was startled out of my dream by Moonbeam, who noticed us lurking in the water. She let out a whinny and started to move in our direction. Bobbie-Lou did not open her eyes, and continued to lie back enjoying the cool water flowing around her and the sun on her face.

"Boo," I said, "Moonbeam saw us. Let's leave."

"Damn, she hasn't stood up yet," he said, but agreed with me. "I want to keep my ears too." We both started to a backward crawl away from Moonbeam. When she saw us retreating, Moonbeam stopped her advance and pawed at the stream bottom.

When we were back to the place where our clothes were, we got out and shook off the water as best we could. We then put our clothes back on. Moonbeam appeared with Bobbie-Lou on her a moment later.

"Let's head for the fort," Boo said.

Boo gave me a boost so that I sat behind Bobbie-Lou. After hoisting Boo up, I wasted no time in putting my hands on Bobbie-Lou's waist.

"Giddyup," Boo said. Moonbeam started her take-off trot, and in an instant, we were headed north, gaining altitude.

Ten

Fort Lyon appeared in the distance on the west side of a creek. It consisted of wooden buildings forming a square about the size of a city block. In the center of the square was a flagpole, flying the same type of flag as Black Kettle had beside his teepee. The only trees were cottonwoods along the bank of the creek. There was a lot of movement in and around the fort. Moonbeam returned to earth a distance away, so we would not be seen flying.

"I'm scared," Bobbie-Lou said as we trotted west over the plains.

"So am I," Boo said.

"Me too," I added. "We've never approached the soldiers to talk before. Teak-qua never said we should do this. Oh well, we'll have to just see what happens."

"What time is it?" Bobbie-Lou asked.

"I don't know," Boo said. "I told you I don't know where my watch is. It wouldn't do any good anyway. The watches always indicated Ohio time. We told you time doesn't have much meaning here."

"It looks like about three or four o'clock, by the sun's position," I said.

"That's as good a guess as any," Boo replied.

We came to the river, but that did not stop Moonbeam. Ordinarily, she would just fly over it, but we saw sentries pointing in our direction, so Moonbeam just started to walk across. The stream was not all that deep; either that, or Moonbeam knew where the rocks were. The water rose only to the bottom of Moonbeam's belly, so when we held our feet up, they never even got wet. When we got to the other side, there were some shrubs and trees to skirt around. After that, it was nothing but dirt to the fort.

We came upon three soldiers on horseback. They were wearing the blue coats, gray pants, and blue caps of the Union Army. My heart started to race as we got closer, and Boo called out to them.

"Where can we find Colonel Chivington?" he said.

"Over yonder in the HQ building," one of the soldiers replied, pointing to one of buildings. He then spit out a stream of tobacco juice through a large, walrus-sized mustache. We couldn't see his mouth through the dense growth, but a little trail of spit clung to the hair and ran down his clean-shaven chin. Bobbie-Lou turned her face away from the crude spectacle. As I was about to get sick, he wiped his chin with the back of his hand. "Are you injuns?"

"No," Boo responded. "We just want to talk to him.

"Well, ya ride bareback like injuns, and ya sure dress funny," one of the other soldiers said. "That horse must have found a shallow spot in the stream, 'cause you hardly got wet. It's about ten feet deep where ya came across."

"That sure is a purdy-lookin' squaw ya got there," one of the other soldiers said.

"I'm no squaw," Bobbie-Lou said. She started to say something else, but I squeezed her waist and, at a whisper, cautioned her to be careful.

"I wasn't talkin' 'bout you, darlin'," he went on. I was talkin' 'bout the one behind ya." All three of them started to laugh.

"Damn queers," I whispered, although I wasn't sure what that really entailed. Our education about homophobic behavior was as limited as our knowledge of heterosexuals.

We ignored their glares as we rode by and headed for the building they indicated as HQ. When we passed in close proximity to them, we got a whiff of what it was like in the Old West when baths were limited to getting wet when your horse forded a deep stream.

We turned around once to see the mustached soldier trying to find the supposed shallow spot where we forded. He prodded his horse to cross where we did. He got about five feet out, and the horse started to swim. Water was up over his saddle before he gave up and headed back to shore. We all three laughed.

Once inside the perimeter of buildings, we passed wagons loaded with boxes that could have contained rifles. The other, smaller boxes in the wagon were most likely ammunition. The only other stationary item in the square area, other than the flagpole, was an open pit. Two men were lighting a large pile of logs. Two others were loading a large side of what must have been buffalo onto a spit.

"Whoa, Moonbeam," Boo said, although she seemed to know where we wanted to go, as if she could interpret the soldier's hand signal. We were in front of a small, wood-sided building with a porch running along the entire front of the structure. There were two windows on either side of a wooden door. A sign beside the door declared this to be the Headquarters of the Third Colorado Calvary, Colonel John M. Chivington, Commanding.

We dismounted, me first, Bobbie-Lou second, and Boo last. We stepped up onto the porch. I led us to the front door. I knocked, and a voice from within said to enter.

When we got through the door, there was a man about twenty-five years old, in a blue uniform, sitting behind a desk. The light coming in through the window to his left illuminated three yellow chevrons on the sleeve of his jacket. There were four wooden, straight-back chairs sitting against the wall to our left. Behind the soldier was a wall with a closed door.

"What do you want?" the soldier asked.

"We would like to see Colonel Chivington," Boo said.

"About what?" he asked.

"We want to talk to him about Black Kettle and the Cheyenne people," I said.

"Well, maybe he don't want to talk to you," was the response we received.

"Who is it?" a booming voice called out from behind the door to the left of the soldier. The soldier got up and walked over to the door.

"Two civilians and a woman," he said through the door. "They want to talk about the injuns over by Sand Creek, colonel, sir."

"A woman, you say? Send them in."

"You'll have to leave your rifles out here," the soldier said. He indicated a rack by the front door. Boo and I put them in the rack and returned to Bobbie-Lou by the desk.

The soldier opened the door and waved his hand, indicating for us to go in. The room we entered was similar to the one we left. Behind a desk, a larger version of the one the soldier had, sat a heavy-set man who looked to be in his mid-forties. His dark but thinning hair stuck out above his ears. It looked like short, thick horns were starting to grow. His beard looked a little like the pictures of Abraham Lincoln, but with a mustache. He had dark, deep-set, coal-black eyes. His uniform was similar to the soldier's, but with two rows of buttons on the chest, and shoulder boards with silver eagles on a yellow field. When he stood up to greet us, he stretched out to over six feet tall.

By the look in his eyes, he is clearly interested in Bobbie-Lou. Boo and I shook his offered hand, but Bobbie-Lou remained mute behind us.

"What can I do for you?" he asks.

"We came for our friends the Cheyenne, and their leader, Black Kettle," I said.

185

"Where are you from?" he asks, ignoring my statement.

"We're from Ohio," Boo said.

"What part?" he continued, staring at Bobbie-Lou. I wanted to reply, *All of us,* but Bobbie-Lou responded before I could let out my smart answer.

"Were from near Akron," she said. We all knew from experience our town was so small, it was not well known.

"I thought I recognized the accent. I was born and raised in Lebanon, close to Cincinnati. I don't know where Akron is."

"It's near Cleveland," I said. I tried to place it near a large city that he would be familiar with.

"Well, sit down, and let's chat," he said, pointing to the four chairs surrounding his desk. After we sat down, he sat back down in his leather chair. His desk was devoid of any objects save some papers, a writing quill, ink well, and blotting paper.

"Are you farm boys?" he asked. "I grew up on a farm. My daddy died when I was five, and me and my brothers had to work the farm to survive." I resisted the urge to correct his grammar. *A military officer should have known better,* I thought.

"As soon as I was ordained a Methodist minister back in '44, I worked my way westward to Denver by way of Missouri and Omaha. You three don't look like you had much of a problem growing up. So why aren't you two boys fightin' the rebels?"

"We aren't old enough yet," I said. I didn't know how old we were supposed to be, but I didn't think we looked eighteen.

"You'll go to hell if your lyin'," he said. "Like I said, I turned down a prayin' position as minister for a fightin' position in the Union Army. I still don't tolerate no liars. I don't tolerate no pro-slavery Southerners neither. If I wasn't needed here to clean Colorado of the Indian menace, I'd be fightin' those secessionist bastards right now. We cleaned all the Confederates out of Colorado, now we need to clean out the injuns. I plan on runnin' for public office as soon as we get statehood. Extermination of the red devils, as the Denver newspaper puts it, is our first priority."

"Well, that's what we came to see you about," I interjected. "Black Kettle and his people are peace loving, and don't want any trouble."

"I'll tell you what I told the governor of Colorado Territory," he said. "The Cheyenne will have to be roundly whipped, or completely wiped out, before they will be quiet. If any of them are caught around here, the only thing to do is kill them."

"They have papers from the president's representative declaring them a friend of the United States," Bobbie-Lou joined in. "Have you no respect for President Lincoln, or any treaties he may have made?"

"Look, young lady," he said. "It is simply not possible for the Indians to understand or obey a treaty. Killing them is the only way we will have peace and quiet in Colorado. Now if you will excuse me, I have some important business to tend to." He rose and walked toward the door, gesturing for us to proceed in front of him.

"Sergeant," he bellowed. "Escort these people away from the fort."

"We can find our own way," Boo said. As soon as the sergeant opened the colonel's door, we heard a commotion outside the building. A horse was whinnying, and several men were shouting. Immediately, I thought Moonbeam was in trouble. Boo and Bobbie-Lou thought the same as we bolted for the door.

We were almost correct. It wasn't Moonbeam who was in trouble; it was the soldiers. Apparently, while we were talking to the colonel, the soldiers decided to take possession of Moonbeam. She did not like it one bit, and had kicked the one who put a rope around her. He was on his side in a heap, holding his gut, while the others scattered in all directions. Moonbeam was menacingly pawing at the grounding.

While Boo and I walked over to Moonbeam to calm her down, Bobbie-Lou retrieved our rifles.

"Well, that was a waste," I said unnecessarily. I grabbed Moonbeam by the rope still hanging from her neck. I lifted it over her head and tossed it to the soldier still clutching his midsection. Moonbeam followed us calmly back to the porch, where we climbed on her back using the existing steps. As Moonbeam walked back toward the entrance to the fort, the scattered soldiers gave a wide berth, letting us pass unopposed. We never even looked back as Moonbeam forded the river in the direction we originally came, never getting wet past our feet.

The same three soldiers watched us cross the stream. As I looked back, I saw one of them scratching his head. We didn't stay around long enough to see whether or not he tried to cross again without getting wet.

"So, what do we do now?" I said over Bobbie-Lou's shoulder.

"I guess we go back and tell Black Kettle what he said," Boo responded.

"I don't think we should say exactly what he said," Bobbie-Lou said. "The part about 'exterminating the red devils' won't go over too well. I think we should tell him not to trust the colonel, and leave it at that."

"You're right," I said. "Let's go, Moonbeam. It's starting to get dark."

Moonbeam started her pre-flight gallop, and was quickly airborne. We said nothing more on the way back. I was wondering about the fate of Black Kettle's people, and was more than a little sad. It would have been nice to "get even" with the Colonel before he inflicted the same damage on the Cheyenne as was done to Nightstar. According to Teak-qua, that was not an option, since we would have no justification. Even if we did get rid of the colonel, there were sure to be others who would take his place. The fate of the Cheyenne and Black Kettle was already settled.

This time, Moonbeam flew right into the camp instead of landing further out and then walking into camp. The Indians looked up as we approached, pointing at us and talking among themselves. Black Kettle soon appeared from his tent, wondering what all the commotion was. Moonbeam put us down right in front of his teepee.

"Now I understand how you knew you could go to the fort so quickly," Black Kettle said. "Teak-qua sent you here on a magical horse. Did you talk to the soldiers?"

"Yes," I said, dismounting. "We talked to Colonel Chivington. He is not a man to be trusted. Is there someone else we can go to?"

"No," Black Kettle said. "We have assurances from all others, but he is the one we must make peace with. You have done all you can and all that we asked. We must await our fate." He turned with his head down and went back in his tent.

Moonbeam bumped her nose into Boo with her we-got-to-get-going nudge.

"I guess it's that time," Boo said. The three of us lined up to mount Moonbeam. The Indians, who were touching her to see if she was real, backed off. Boo got on first, and Bobbie-Lou and I followed. The Indians watched in awe as we climbed toward the heavens. The sun was just setting in the west. Boo and I had seen the spectacle before, but still stared in amazement.

"That is the most beautiful sight I've ever seen," Bobbie-Lou said.

"Yes, it is," I sighed over her shoulder. It seemed as though Moonbeam understood our appreciation of the sunset, because she circled several times before speeding up to the present. This time Bobbie-Lou rode very relaxed in front of me. I again placed my hands on her hips with a reassuring grip. Her head swung slowly side to side, looking at the streaks the stars made. As we slowed down, the moon magically appeared, first in a blur, and then still and sharp. Moonbeam approached the first tee at the country club.

I dismounted, but Bobbie-Lou sat a little longer on Moonbeam. She finally reluctantly got down, and Boo followed. She then looked down at her chest and noticed she had reverted back to her pre-trip size. She also looked at her rear end to notice its change also. There was a little pout on her face as she looked back at us.

"That was incredible," she said, after a moment. "I can't wait to go back again." She gave Moonbeam a hug and a kiss on the nose, which I watched with envy.

Were not taking you back, I thought. *I'm afraid the next trip is going to be nasty.*

"When will we go back?" she asked.

"We don't know," Boo said. "Sometimes it's the next day. Sometimes it's a week later. Just be ready anytime."

Bobbie-Lou did all the talking on our walk back to her house. She went on about the flying, the way everyone was dressed, and of course, the sunset. Boo and I let her ramble. I was picturing some of the horror we witnessed on previous trips.

When we got to Bobbie-Lou's house, the screen was still propped up against the brick exterior under her window. Boo and I both helped her up and in with a two-man hand lift, although she was not that heavy. When she reached out to get the screen from me, she gave me a little hug around the neck and a kiss on the nose, just like she gave Moonbeam. I watched as she positioned the screen in its recess and slipped the retainers back in place. I finally left her looking out from behind the screen, when Boo tugged at me breaking my trance.

We sneaked back along the fences to our fort. Teak-qua was waiting for us.

"Did your friend have a good trip?" Teak-qua asked.

"She enjoyed it," Boo said.

"Good. The next trip is tomorrow night. I don't think you want to take her with you this time. It will be very dangerous."

"Will it be as bad as when Nightstar was killed?" I asked.

"Worse," he said, and started to chant.

I crawled into my sleeping bag and pulled the top half over my head. I tried to hide the same way I hid after my dad took our family to see *The Thing from Another World* at the drive-in movie three years before. James Arness as The Thing scared me to death. I hid under the covers the rest of that summer as I visualized the severed hand pounding on a table. Finally I fell asleep to Teak-qua's rhythmic chanting.

Eleven

We were awakened by the snap of a twig.

"Who's out there?" I whispered to Boo.

"I don't know," he said. "I hope it's not Pinky." Then we saw Skubini's face, followed by David's, peering in the dark recess of the fort. David had on his I'm-mister-cool, State Street Junior High, blue and gold jacket over his white T-shirt. He started junior high last year and was proud of it. He wore the jacket when it was ninety degrees in the shade. I swear he must have slept in it. David wore his hair greased up, with a spit curl in front and a DA (duck's ass) in the back. He must have been the poster boy for "The Fonz" on the TV show *Happy Days*.

Skubini had on a white T-shirt too, and like David wore "genuine Levis." They were the more expensive blue jeans that showed the blue stripe when the pant leg was rolled up. Boo and I always got a knock-off brand that did not have the blue stripe. I longed for the day when I could afford a pair of genuine Levis with the blue stripe. Later in life when I could afford to buy my own, rolling up your pant leg had long been out of style. Both were in sneakers, like us.

"You guys in there?" David said.

"Yeah," I said, grabbing for a cigarette. "You scared the crap out of us. We thought you were Pinky."

"Hey, give me one of those," Skubini said, reaching for my stolen pack of Marlboro's.

"Help yourself," I said. *He always was a moocher. Why doesn't he steal his own cigarettes?* David never did smoke. The only reason I could figure out was that they cost too much, and he was saving for a car as soon as he turned sixteen. If he had smoked, he would have kept them rolled up in his T-shirt sleeve. If he didn't have that damn jacket, that is.

"Your mom's gonna smell those on you," David said. Neither of Skubini's parents smoked, so they would know if he came home smelling of cigarettes. One time he chewed on grass to get rid of the smell on his breath. He had me do the same thing, but I almost threw up, so never did it again. My dad smoked, and our whole house smelled so bad, they would never detect it on me.

"My parents went to Toledo this morning," Skubini said. "My aunt had a baby last night, so they left me and Janet home alone." Janet was Skubini's sister, already about to graduate from the Catholic High School, so of no interest to us. Besides, she was as homely looking as Linda.

"We're going to build a go-cart," David said. "Wanna help?" David's "wanna help" meant he needed someone to help him finance his venture.

"Sure," Boo said. "I need to go home and get some breakfast first."

"Me too," I said.

"Okay," David said. "Meet us in Skubini's garage after you eat." Boo was rummaging around in the back of the cave, and finally came up with his Roy Rogers watch, the one he leant to Teak-qua.

"What's that on the back wall?" Skubini asked.

"Some old bones," I said. I did not want to bring anymore of the neighborhood in on our little secret. It was bad enough that Bobbie-Lou knew first hand, and Linda was told. Bobbie-Lou was sworn to secrecy, and Linda didn't believe us. But, if Bobbie-Lou blabbed about last night's trip to Linda, the whole town would know by nightfall, including my nosy sisters. Then my parents would know, and my dad was sure to investigate.

"Yeah, some old bones," Boo said. Apparently he too did not want Skubini and David to know.

"Let's go," I said, and made a movement toward the fort entrance. David and Skubini backed up and out, and Boo and I followed.

After breakfast, which for me was a self-made peanut butter and jelly sandwich chased down with some skim milk, I headed for Skubini's.

When I got there, Skubini and David already had the framework for the cart laid out on the garage floor. Four two-by-fours salvaged from discarded Grove Refrigeration shipping pallets would make up the body of the cart.

We used to get a lot of stuff from Grove's. We were able to create buildings from refrigerator boxes discarded by Grove Refrigeration. We would ride by Grove's back door almost daily, scouting for the wood-framed, cellulose-clad, giant Lego blocks we would use in constructing our cardboard condominiums. Finding one, we would race home as fast as our peanut butter-fueled legs would propel our second-hand Schwinn Phantoms, grab our little red wagons, and head to Grove's to collect our treasure.

Hauling a forty-four-cubic-foot, flimsy refrigerator box with a one-by-two, little red wagon the five blocks from Grove's to the edge of the Watson Woods, was an engineering feat only duplicated by the Egyptians building the great pyramids. Finally, though, we would get the building block to the construction site, where there were two to three other units awaiting another room. Last summer's construction project involved five boxes proudly advertising Kelvinator on one side, and on the other side, "this end up" pointing in a northerly or southerly direction. It was bad karma to place a refrigerator box pointing east and west.

Trap doors interconnected the rooms to the condo where we placed our sleeping bags, Spider-man comic books, transistor radio, and flashlights for our sleep-outs. We also had window flaps on the sides and ends to open when we heard saber-toothed mice rummaging around at night. We spent many a summer night in those cardboard condos, which barely measured two feet, top to bottom.

So what happened to our cardboard condos? Five boxes, two high, side by side with a penthouse on top, was the most we ever amassed before a summer downpour converted our playhouse into a brown clump of papier-mâché and sticks. We used a tarp to cover the roof, but that did not protect the soft underbelly and flimsy sides. Eventually the whole thing collapsed into what looked like what a log-eating monster would pass through its system, digesting all but the hard, inner core of the many trees it ate.

In time, this pile of monster feces would dry up enough where we could drag it out from under the trees to a clearing we called a burn pit. That was when our refrigerator boxes provided another round of fun. Our neighbors didn't think it was fun when they looked out their kitchen window to see a bonfire the size of Rhode Island just twenty feet from their 1954 Packard, with hydraulic leveling and bright yellow and black paint blistering from the heat. Today's refrigerator boxes don't have any wood framing like they used to. It's a good thing too.

So, they had the framework laid out. Boo had walked in while I was inspecting the other items on the garage floor. There were two lawn mower engines off to the side, along with other parts saved from previous year's go-carts. I recognized one of the engines as the one Skubini and I used last year to motorize my bike. We had built a platform with plywood and wheels from my little red wagon. We bolted a pulley to the wheel. The motor was bolted to the platform. A V-belt connected the pulley on the motor to the one on the wheel. We used some steel bars to attach the platform to the bike axles. A string allowed the rider to control the throttle.

It was a simple device, but not a good design. The engine was started by peddling or being pushed. Once the engine caught fire, you pulled on the string to go. Applying the brakes stopped the engine. It only worked on a couple of trial runs. By then, the rear axle on my bike was stripped, and had to be replaced. We scrapped the motor-bike idea and stuck with go-carts.

David had a centrifugal clutch, which was the most expensive part of the go-cart. That meant the engine could be running at idle and the cart would be stopped. When the throttle was increased, then the clutch engaged and the cart started to move. What was unique about David's new design was the use of two engines. To compensate for the different speeds the two engines might operate at, David decided to have them connected by pulleys to one shaft. That shaft would have the centrifugal clutch that would be connected to the wheel-shaft pulley. Since pulleys were cheap, and centrifugal clutches were not, only one expensive clutch was needed.

Steering was by use of a wooden dowel from an old broom handle, and some rope. The dowel rod was secured at both ends so that it was allowed to rotate. The rope was coiled around the rod and attached to the front-wheel axles. When the rod was twisted with the steering wheel (a board nailed to the driver's end) this simple machine tightened the rope on one side while letting out slack on the other, thus aiming the wheels.

Other go-carts had always used the wheels from little red wagons that we outgrew, or discarded lawn mowers, which also provided engines. The wheels never lasted very long because they had bushings instead of bearings to absorb the heat caused by spinning friction against the axle. The brass bushings wore thin after a week's hard use, no matter how much oil was squirted on them. Then the wheels just flopped around and were useless. Dangerous was not a word in our vocabulary. For this go-cart, David had acquired four wheels with bearings.

By afternoon, we had all the components assembled. It was ready for a test run. David filled one of the gas tanks, but ran out of gas.

"No problem," Skubini said. "I have some here in the garage we can use."

When Skubini was done filling the second engine's tank, it was time for a test run. The first engine was started with the pull rope. Because the engines were connected, when the one engine fired, it started the other engine. White smoke billowed out from the second engine's exhaust and filled the garage. When David got the engines stopped, and the smoke cleared somewhat, Boo looked at the can from which Skubini poured the contents into the second gas tank.

"It's kerosene," Boo exclaimed.

"No wonder it smoked," I said. David was a little pissed, but kept calm.

"I'll get it out of the tank," Skubini said. He then started to take off the gas tank so he could empty its contents back into the kerosene tank.

"I'll go get some gas from our garage," Boo said, and headed across the street to his house. Billows of dense white smoke were cascading out of the open garage door.

"What's going on?" Bobbie-Lou asked, as she walked from her backyard to Skubini's adjacent garage. "My mom saw all the smoke and thought something was on fire. She called the fire department." This last bit of information was unnecessary because just then, we could hear the sirens on their way from the fire station two blocks away.

"Hide the go-cart," David said in a panic. We had been stopped by the police before for riding the carts in the street. We only got a warning then, but the cops were sure to be with the fire truck and they might take the cart if they saw it. While I helped David push the cart out of the garage, a quick-thinking Skubini poured some kerosene into his dad's lawn mower and started it up. Smoke again filled the garage, billowing out from the door. The smoke provided a screen, hiding David, me, and the cart as we pushed it out the front and around the side of the garage. Just as we got to the back of the garage, the fire department pulled up at the curb. Skubini turned off the lawn mower as the first fireman, in full gear, came up the driveway.

Bobbie-Lou, leaning against the garage with her hands folded, was watching our Keystone Kops antics with amazement.

David and I covered the cart with a tarp we found behind the garage, and calmly walked back around to where Skubini was showing the fireman the offending lawn mower. Bobbie-Lou was looking at David and me, with her arms still folded and a frown on her face. David held one finger up to his lips, begging her to be quiet. The fireman picked up the can sitting beside the lawnmower.

"Here's the problem," the fireman said to the second arriving fireman, who was also in full gear. "You put kerosene in the tank, not gasoline." They both laughed a little as Skubini tried to look as puzzled as ever.

"Next time, read the label on the can, and be careful," the second fireman said. "When you clean out the gas tank, do it outside the garage and make sure there aren't any flames nearby. You boys behave now." He directed the comment to David and me, as well as Skubini. I saw Boo starting across the street with a can of gas, and waved my hand at him from the hip, warning him to stay put.

Bobbie-Lou did her best silent "upidstay oybays" with a shake of her head, turned around, and headed back to her house. Neighbors, who were all non-working mothers, were watching the proceedings from their porches. When the firemen returned calmly to their truck and took off their fire-fighting slickers, the neighborhood returned to normal. The old lady would have a lot to tell Der Captain when he got home from work.

When the fire truck had departed, Boo resumed his trek across the street, can of gas in hand. David and I retrieved the go-cart. Skubini emptied the lawn mower tank by tipping it on its side by the edge of the driveway.

"That's gonna leave a brown spot," David said.

"Well, I couldn't put it back in the can," Skubini said. "Gas was mixed with the kerosene."

Boo filled the second tank, and we started both the engines, this time with just a little smoke until the kerosene burned away. An anxious David hopped in the driver's seat and pulled on the string accelerator. The cart leapt to action and took off down the driveway. Without stopping, David swung it to the right and toward the south end of Watson. He was lucky no cars were coming. We ran down the driveway to watch. When we got there, he was turning it around and heading back toward Skubini's house. He was flying as he turned to come back up the driveway, only he was going so fast, he slid into a parked car. Luckily he hit the tire and did no damage to the car, but the cart and David were not so lucky.

David sprained an ankle, and spent most of the next week getting around by peddling his bike with one foot. The engines had ripped loose from the hold-down bolts. The wood holding the steering mechanism was busted in two, and so was the dowel rod. It took most of the next morning to fix the cart. David did not ride it in the street anymore, but we towed it with my bike to an empty parking lot for a safer ride.

That night, Boo and I stayed in the fort. We awoke this time to the smell of Teak-qua's pipe. He was silent as he watched us gather our BB guns and canvas bags. We had a half-finished, quart mason jar of homemade elderberry jelly that we had on graham crackers before we went to sleep. There was enough for a treat for Moonbeam, so the jar went into the canvas bag. I heard the click as the jar hit against the signal mirror that Boo put in previously. He pulled the jar out and gave it me, to keep one from breaking the other. I put the jar in my bag while Boo looked at his wrist to make sure he was wearing his watch.

"My braves," Teak-qua said. "Are you ready to go on anther trip?"

"Yes," Boo said. "But we're not taking any girls with us this time."

"That is wise," he said. "You will see some bad things being done to Black Kettle's people. It is good your friend will not be along. You will also not come back until your work is done. Do not forget your rifles. Now go. Moonbeam awaits."

"Where is she this time?" I asked.

"She will find you."

Moonbeam did find us. She picked us up on Cherry Avenue as we emerged from the woods in the same place Teak-qua came out on the way to the movies. We quickly got on her back, dreading what was in store for us.

She shot through space and time as before, and entered the past at the same creek where the Cheyenne were still camped. It was early morning. The Rocky Mountains in the distance were covered in snow, almost to their base. The rising sun in the east tinted the snow pink. Moonbeam swooped low and was getting dangerously close to some trees.

"We're gonna hit the trees," Boo said, from his perch behind me.

"Moonbeam," I said, "what are you doing?"

I don't know if she heard me or not, but she headed right for the middle of a large cottonwood along the banks of the Sand Creek. Boo and I ducked down behind her head, expecting to be smashed to bits. Instead, we passed right through the tree, as if it were a shadow. We passed through two more trees before I had the nerve to sit straight again.

"Boo! Boo!" I exclaimed. "We're invisible. We went right through those trees. Moonbeam is showing us that we can't be seen."

Boo sat up, after he saw I was still in one piece.

"Holy cow," he said. "We are passing right through the trees."

"Yeah, it's cool, ain't it?"

I held out my hand as we passed close to another cottonwood. I watched as my hand and arm went through without a scratch. Boo did the same on the next tree.

"I wonder why we are invisible this time?" I asked, but then it came to me. "We're going to be there when the bad things happen. We're invisible so we won't be hurt too." Moonbeam whinnied as if in agreement of my observation.

"I get it," Boo said. "Moonbeam couldn't tell us, so she had to show us."

"I just said that a minute ago." Moonbeam broke away from the creek and headed back in the direction of the Cheyenne's camp. By this time, the sun was up. I looked down at the ground. As far as I could tell, we were not casting a shadow. This was confirmed as soon as we got to the edge of the camp and Moonbeam landed. There were shadows from the teepees, but none from us.

Boo and I stayed quiet as we moved among the Indians. They were starting their day, getting out of the teepees to greet the warming rays of the morning sun. We did not know if they could hear us if we talked, so we did not try. If we said something and we were invisible, we could scare them. I listened for the sound of

Moonbeam's hooves on the ground, but heard none. That was not unusual, because she rarely made a noise.

I noticed that there were not many braves in the camp. I counted maybe thirty or forty, but hundreds of women and children. The rest must have been out hunting buffalo. I saw Black Kettle and White Antelope walking together near Black Kettle's teepee. Moonbeam headed back out to the perimeter of the camp. In the distance, we could see soldiers coming from the direction of Fort Lyon. When they got closer, they formed a semicircle around the camp from the northern edge of the creek to the southern. They wheeled up four canons to their front lines and aimed them toward the Cheyenne.

We watched the developing storm from atop Moonbeam while walking around the perimeter of the camp. A lone figure appeared, walking out from the camp. I urged Moonbeam in that direction, so we could see who it was.

As soon as I recognized him, I whispered, "White Antelope." My voice had a strange timbre to it, almost a vibrato.

"It is," came back Boo. His voice sounded the same, as if we were ghosts in a bad dream. When we said this, we were beside White Antelope. He did not act like he heard us.

We walked alongside him to within fifty feet of the soldiers. The soldiers raised their guns and aimed directly at him. White Antelope began to chant as the Blue Coats fired, tearing him apart. We were startled, but did not move an inch. Boo raised his rifle over my shoulder and fired. The sound the gun made was like an echo.

We could see the bullet exit the waves of air that surrounded us, and then just disappear. The accompanying puff of smoke did the same.

"That was a waste," Boo gargled.

"It might have just provoked the soldiers if you would have hit one of them," I gargled back.

White Antelope was obviously dead, so we turned around and headed back to the encampment. As we were heading back, something passed right through us on its way into the mass of teepees. When it exploded, we realized it was a shell from one of the canons. Boo and I turned our heads around to see the other three canons belching smoke. They were so close, they fired almost horizontally into the camp. We turned, facing the Indians in time to see more explosions. Moonbeam continued into the center of the camp as more shells exploded around us. We were not injured, as shell fragments passed right through our bodies, causing nothing more than a ripple. The Indians were not as lucky. Some were lifted up by the explosions; some were pierced by the metal that passed so harmlessly through our ghost of a vision.

In the center of the camp, Black Kettle had raised the flag the commissioner had given him. Alongside the American flag was a white flag of peace. Believing what the commissioner told him, that no one would fire upon anyone standing under the stars and stripes, Black Kettle was gathering his people around the two flags. It did no good. The shells kept coming, exploding, killing, injuring.... We counted less than forty braves who were able to fight back, but it was a futile effort against overwhelming odds.

Right through the horrified Cheyenne, Moonbeam took us back to the edge of the camp. A few minutes later, when the shelling stopped, the soldiers amassed a charge. Colonel Chivington was in front of the pack. He raised his arm, sword in hand, and then dropped it, pointing toward the camp. We noticed more than a few of the soldiers had trouble getting on their horses. They acted like the drunken actors we saw in some movies at the Strand. Once on their horses, though, they followed the others charging on the innocent women and children, firing indiscriminately. All of the armed braves had been killed as the first wave of soldiers entered the camp. Now the soldiers charged on the mass of Indians huddled around the flags. When it was inevitable that the Blue Coats were headed in their direction, the ones who could scampered for the unguarded creek. More than half made it across, including Black Kettle. The rest were outnumbered two to one.

Moonbeam meandered through the slaughter that was taking place. With no opposition, the soldiers shot anyone standing. They then dismounted. In frenzy, they started clubbing women and children with the butts of their guns. The mutilation was terrible. Some of the soldiers had a bottle of rye whiskey in their hands, taking a drink in between atrocities. When they were busy cutting open the bellies of women, they passed the bottle to their fellow soldiers. We saw one child of four or five pleading for his life over the mutilated corpse of his mother. The drunken soldier standing over him clubbed him to death.

As we watched in horror, unable to assist, the soldiers continued for an hour with their mutilations. They took scalps, both head and body, and hung them from their swords as trophies. By the time the slaughter had ended, Moonbeam was wading in blood. The soldiers scattered all the Cheyenne's horses and mules, in addition to mutilating the dead and dying Indians.

"Moonbeam, can we please leave," I pleaded, still in a garbled tone. She thankfully led us away. I wanted to throw up, but didn't. The mutilations were similar to what we found had been done to Hunts Bear's people, and Nightstar. The difference was we did not witness that event. We were out of sight of the camp and the soldiers before the color returned to my face.

"I can't wait to get even with the colonel," Boo said. His voice sounded normal. We noticed that Moonbeam was now going around the trees instead of through them.

"I think we can be seen again," I said, also sounding normal.

"Look, there are our shadows," Boo said, pointing to our right. "We must be visible again."

Twelve

To our surprise, Moonbeam took flight. She circled the area for a while, and then sped up. Soon we were in the shooting stars, but instead forming a straight line as before, they spun in a circle around us. When we slowed down and the stars became pinpoints of light again and the moon was a big, round, shiny globe, it was dark. We had no idea where we were, until I spotted in the distance the same Rocky Mountains from our last trip. The bright moonlight illuminated the snow at the very tops of the peaks. We were a lot closer than before.

"It must be summer or spring," I said. To confirm this, we landed in a field of wildflowers. We stayed on Moonbeam's back as she made her way westerly toward the mountain peeks. When she stopped, the dark-blue color of morning formed an arc in the east.

Ahead of us, illuminated by the still, bright moon and the morning light of dawn on a flat plain, was a cabin. There was a smaller building in the back, which looked like the outhouse, and a corral with horses in it. We dismounted and walked over to the horses. Moonbeam was with us, and somehow was communicating with them, for they came over to see her. None of them made a noise. Eight saddles were on the top rail of the split-rail fence. I counted the same number of horses. The saddles were the same military type we saw at Fort Lyon and during the attack at Sand Creek.

A saddlebag on one of the saddles caught my eye, so I went to it for a closer look.

Colonel J. M. Chivington was engraved on the side of one saddle, next to crossed swords and a U.S. insignia.

"He's here," I whispered to Boo. "Here is his saddle."

Boo came to have a look, shook his head, and said, "Yeah, it's gotta be him. They must be on a scouting mission, looking for more Indians to butcher."

We wondered what to do next. We had no dynamite, no carbide tablets, and no rocket fuel. All we had for our arsenal were our rifles, a signal mirror, and the half-full mason jar.

"I forgot to give that to Moonbeam," Boo said. I handed the jar to him. He took the lid off and held it out for her. Her long tongue made quick work of the rest of the elderberry jelly. He put the two-piece lid back on the jar when it was licked clean. While he was feeding Moonbeam, he was thinking out loud.

"All we can do is shoot them," Boo said. "How can we get them all out at once? If they come out one at a time, they'll see Moonbeam and us. If we shoot them before they're all out, then we can't surprise the rest of them.

"I don't know," I said, but a plan was coming to me. "Remember how we used to trap the bees in a jar and throw the jar at my sisters? When the jar broke, the bees would come out really mad."

"We got a jar," Boo said, "but we got no bees."

We both looked around the meadow we were standing in. In the early morning, there was plenty of dew and wildflowers, but the bees had not yet ventured out.

"We can't wait until the sun comes up and the bees come out," I said.

"Wait a minute," an excited Boo said. "Look at the roof on the outhouse. That looks like a hornet nest hanging from the back corner." We laid our rifles against the fence and walked in the direction of the outhouse.

I squinted as both of us moved even closer. It was a paper-looking ball with hornets hanging from it. In the cool and dark of the morning, the hornets were not very active. The nest was a little smaller than the mason jar we had. If we missed, and the hornets became angry, there was hell to pay for us. On the other hand, a bunch of angry hornets in the cabin would get the men out in a hurry, and probably without their rifles.

Boo and I carefully sneaked up on the nest. The hornets did not seem interested in us. I opened the jar, being careful to make sure the two-piece lid stayed together. Boo backed away as I reached up with the lid in my left hand and the jar in my right hand. I slipped the jar up and over the nest trapping all against the eave of the roof. The hornets now noticed us and were starting to emerge from the ball.

Holy shit, I thought. *If I don't get the lid on in the first try, I'll get the shit stung out of me. Hail Mary, full of grace....*

"Slide the jar to the side, and the ball will detach from the roof," Boo suggested.

I did so, and the ball detached, dropping to the bottom of the jar. The hornets, however, were all over the inside. I handed Boo the lid. If this was going to go bad, we were both going to suffer.

"Take the top part of the lid and hold against the roof while I slide the jar to the side and under it," I instructed. "Then let go." Boo did what I told him, and soon we had the lid between the jar and the roof. I held out my hand, never taking my eyes from the buzzing jar. "Now, put the screw part over my hand and down onto my wrist." My right arm was tiring, but now with the rest of the lid over my fingers, I carefully reached up, tilted the jar slightly to one side, and held the flat part tightly to the jar with my left hand.

As I lowered my arms, I told Boo, whose eyes were as big and round as golf balls, to slide the screw part up my hand and over the lip of the jar and turn it tightly into place. When he had finished that, I took what must have been my first breath in minutes and checked the tightness of the lid. Satisfied, I handed the jar to Boo. He held it up to within and inch of his face and looked at the now very active hornets. I stuck my hands in my pockets to relieve the shakiness as we walked back to Moonbeam to retrieve our rifles.

"Okay, kemosabe," I said. "Now all we have to do is get the hornets in the cabin and get 'em as they run out for cover." At that, we picked up our rifles and headed back to the cabin, approaching from the east side, where there were no doors and one window open to the breaking morning sun. The sun was low and to our backs. If anyone looked out of the window, toward us, the light would blind them.

Our plan was simple: Boo would break for the front south corner of the cabin while I readied the hornet bomb near the window. He would use the signal mirror when he was in place and ready. I would unscrew the lid and toss the jar through the window. If the jar did not break, at least the hornets would find their way out when the dome fell off. I would then run to the back north corner of the cabin and nail anyone who came out the north and east exits. Boo would holler if he had too many targets to shoot at. I would do the same, but odds were most of the soldiers would come out the front.

"Go," I whispered to Boo. "I'll wait for your signal, and then toss the hornets in." Boo took off, crouching as he moved quickly around the southeast corner of the cabin.

About a minute or two later, I got the flash of light from the mirror. I moved to the window, unscrewed the lid, raised up, and tossed the bomb in the open window, doing my best John Wayne grenade-lobbing toss. It was a good one, and the jar must have traveled to the other side of the cabin before thudding against the dirt floor. There was a muffled tink tink as the lid fell off. It was a good thing I removed the screw band, because the dirt floor kept the jar from breaking.

"What the hell was that?" one of the soldiers said in an obviously just-woke-up voice.

"Holy shit!" one of the other soldiers yelled.

"Ow! Damn, ow!" yet another hollered.

I heard the front door slam open against the outside wall. This was followed by a shot, hopefully from Boo. Then another shot, and another. I was watching the back when I glanced back toward the window I threw the bomb into. A soldier in red long johns was crawling out with a pistol in his left hand. He was swatting at a hornet with his right. I let him get all the way out while I glanced around the back of the building to make sure no one had left by that means. When I turned back toward the armed soldier, he was looking in my direction and transferring the pistol to his right hand. I quickly aimed and fired a shot, which caught him in the shoulder and spun him around. Another shot and his head exploded in a gory mess all over the side of the cabin.

I had no time to get sick, as a bullet whizzed past my right ear and buried itself in the outhouse over my left shoulder. I dropped to the ground, and in a prone position fired in the direction of the rear of the cabin, missing the naked soldier who fired at me. I was lucky he was now busy swatting at a swarm of angry hornets. He was not able to get off another shot as I fired into his right side, knocking him off his feet. I then fired a shot right at his groin. The bullet must have gone right up his ass because shit flew back toward me. That was when I heard Boo holler for help.

Seeing no more soldiers in my area, I went to the back of the cabin and peered in. There were no soldiers inside, and the hornets must have found their way out, chasing the hollering men. I ran through the cabin and carefully looked out the front door. Two soldiers in their red long johns had Boo pinned down behind a wagon. One of them was Chivington. They were firing mercilessly,

214

and Boo could not get off a returning shot. I aimed and fired just as Moonbeam ran over to get Boo out. I hit the soldier to Boo's right in the back of the head, killing him instantly, but Chivington got off a shot which would have hit Boo, but instead caught Moonbeam in her left flank.

She did not go down, but staggered. I was really pissed now and fired at the colonel. I hit him as he turned to see where I was. It got him in the gut. He dropped his rifle, and on the run I shot him in the shoulder. I ran to Moonbeam as Boo got up.

"Did you see anyone else?" I asked.

"No," Boo said. "I think we got them all. I had six here." I looked around and verified the count. Not one of the soldiers, except the colonel, was moving.

"I got two, so that must be all of them." We both went to Moonbeam, who was favoring her left hind leg. She was bleeding profusely from the wound, but she was nudging us to get on her back.

"Oh Moonbeam," I said. "Poor girl. Can you get us out of here?"

"I hope she can," Boo responded. "Otherwise we are in a world of hurt. We're stuck here forever." I looked in Chivington's direction. He was not dead, but would be soon. He was holding his gut, blood pouring out from between his fingers. He was obviously hurting from his wounds.

Moonbeam shook her head up and down to answer my question, so Boo and I jumped on her back. If a horse could wince, Moonbeam did so. She was able to start moving, although with a bad limp. It took her longer than normal to get us off the ground. We circled the cabin one time. Chivington was writhing in pain.

"I hope you suffer all the way to hell," I yelled at him, as we headed for the heavens and back to our time. Unlike other trips back, the ride seemed longer, and a few times it seemed as though we hesitated. Both of us kept checking Moonbeam's wound. Blood covered her left rear leg and ran in a streak down and under her belly. Moonbeam normally held her head high as we traversed the time zones, but this time her head was bowed.

Just like the previous trip, when we got back to the fort, Teak-qua was sitting cross-legged, eyes closed, near the entrance. He was smoking his pipe and chanting. The night air was heavy with fog.

"Teak-qua," I said, hoping to get his attention. He did not look at us. We sidestepped him and moved to the middle of the fort. We were both shaking as we laid our BB guns down and sat beside them on our bags.

"Teak-qua!" Boo shouted. He opened his eyes this time.

"Moonbeam was shot," I said, trying unsuccessfully to fight back a tear. "She may be dead by now; she was able to drop us off over on Cherry, but then she took off by herself. She was losing a lot of blood, and her head was drooping." By this time there was a tremor in my voice.

"Moonbeam has returned to her ancestral home," Teak-qua said. "She does not feel any pain, and is happy."

"Well, shit, were not," Boo added. Although I did not look at him, I sensed Boo had tears welling up also.

"What is wrong, my warriors?" he asked.

"This time we got shot at," I said, anger replacing my sorrow. "We could have gotten killed, or if Moonbeam had, we would be stuck in the past, shit out of luck." *Hail Mary, full of grace...,* I thought, to atone for my swearing.

"Yeah," added Boo. "I don't know about you, Andy, but I'm through with this happy horseshit stuff. It was fun at first, but I don't want to die. Besides, I'm not so sure the Indians were so innocent."

"What do you mean?" Teak-qua asked, his head cocked to one side.

Oh shit, I thought. *Now we've pissed off the Indians.*

"There were a lot of killings on both sides," Boo said. "I know we saw the Indian's side of things, but we didn't see the way the Indians killed the white people."

"Of course, there were killings on both sides," Teak-qua said. "The white man was not totally at fault. But my race was always punished far more than the white man was. The first settlers of America were the Indians. The white man invaded us with their modern weapons, which we could not fight against with bows and arrows. You will not find in your history books the way the Indians were captured and used as slaves. The ones who survived caught the white man's diseases. Entire villages and tribes were wiped out. The white man robbed the graves to take whatever was buried with our dead. They stole our grain, burned our houses, and took over the fields we cleared and planted for centuries. That is why so many New England towns end in field. Indian women would abandon their babies to flee the pursuing white man. Then those that were left were forced into slavery or killed."

"No," I said, "we were not taught that."

"The Thanksgiving," Teak-qua continued, "that you were told about never happened. Corn, squash, cranberries, and turkey were all provided by or shown how to be grown by the Indians. These foods are what allowed the European invaders to survive the fierce New England winters. Only after we found out how to use the white man's weapons, did the surviving Indians fight back. In the process, we had to give up the way we lived for centuries. We are now forced to live the way the white man wants us to live. We never had one way to live before the white man came. We had many ways, which were constantly changing. Now, to salvage what little we have left in a way of life and our heritage, we must be confined to reservations, go to white man's schools, accept white man's food, accept white man's medicine. The lands where our ancestors were buried are sacred and hallowed grounds to us. We have been forced to abandon them, or relocate the remains when found. We are still suffering for what we did, but the men who suffered injustices to us, did not get punished.

"You have helped to affect a small measure of revenge for my people, and for that we thank you. I hope that now you will seek both sides to the story, and not accept what you read in school, or what you see at the movies. Remember the mistakes of the past, and do not foster the conviction that Europeans and their descendants are superior to all others and force their beliefs, religion, and government on other races. If you do, you will always be at war, and needless deaths will result. Above all, be tolerant of others and love them as brothers. Remember this lesson and your lives will be happy and fulfilling.

"I will not ask you to take anymore trips. I would only ask you to continue your lives, knowing that you have experienced a great adventure. I will not see you again until we meet in the afterlife. And I can say that for both of you, our reunion will be a long time from now."

"What happened to Black Kettle?" I asked. "He escaped across the river with some of the Cheyenne."

"He was killed, along with his wife, in another massacre four years later."

"Will we see Moonbeam again?" I asked.

"You will see her as often as you like," Teak-qua responded. "In your day and night dreams, and yes, when the time comes, you will be with her again. I must leave you now. Thank you again for what you have done, and also thank you for the visit to the dream house, and your gift of tobacco."

With that said, Teak-qua stood up and walked away from the entrance to the fort. He did not go down the hill as Mugsy's rock had, but stepped into the mist and was gone.

"Good-bye, Teak-qua," I said, with heavy eyelids. Boo was already lying flat on his bag and sound asleep. It had been a hard and exhausting night for both of us. As I too lay down on my bag, I fell asleep wondering if this was a dream. Would I remember this tomorrow? Then I did dream.

In my dream, I became aware of Teak-qua, similar to the other times. Teak-qua was chanting. His pipe was lit and held in his left hand. The smoke, drifting up from the tobacco, cast a cloud in the semi-dark cave. I blinked myself to awareness, but instead of speaking, I was mesmerized by the words, or lack of them, coming from Teak-qua. Although I was able to understand the other Indians in previous trips to the past, the words in the chant were from an ancient language, as old as man. I blinked again, and then again. Teak-qua was transparent. Through his body, I could see the back of the wall, quivering, not so much from the flicker of the campfire or the wafting pipe smoke, but from the carnival-like gossamer of his body.

Teak-qua. My thoughts floated with the rhythm of the chant. *Teak-qua, do you want me to ride again?* No response. *Teak-qua, may I fly with Moonbeam one more time?* No response. *I miss Moonbeam. She was a good friend. Can she take me to the future? Can she ride ahead in time, as well as back?* In an eternity of dream time, I waited for a response. In actual time it was probably a split second before I got one.

Why do you want to ride to the future? In that same lilting, chanting tone, Teak-qua's thoughts floated back to me. *The future is a dangerous place. Much more dangerous than the past. I can send you with Moonbeam, but you can only observe, and only by yourself. You cannot change the future, by will or action. Do you understand?*

Yes. I want to be with Moonbeam one more time.

What you see will remain with you, but deep in your mind. The thoughts may surface, but it will seem like a dream, nothing more. He put the pipe to his lips and inhaled deeply. Exhaling a blue-white storm of smoke toward me, his thoughts bade me, *Now go, if you dare. Moonbeam awaits.*

When the smoke cleared, I was on the island where we first met Moonbeam. I saw Moonbeam standing in front of me. She was a glowing, silvery mass, like liquid crystal. There was a scar on her left flank where she had been shot. Instead of walking, I floated over to her, and we became one. A horse and rider appearing in the same shimmering, ghostly translucency Teak-qua had in the cave.

Moonbeam took flight, but there were no stars, no moon, nothing to guide our journey. We traveled in total darkness, until a pinpoint of light far ahead started to grow. There were hazy, green objects moving by on the right. I strained to see what they were. One after the other, the green objects passed by. I was able to see them more clearly as the light became larger. *They are words. No numbers,* I thought. *Groups of numbers. Four numbers at a time.* I was able to make out one of them. The pinpoint of light had grown, filling almost a fourth of the sky.

1-9-9-0, I read. *1-9-9-1* was the next. *It's years, the numbers are years.* The green numbers kept passing by. *1994, 1995.* The sky was half filled with light. *1996.* Then, no more numbers. We emerged from the tunnel of darkness into the dawn of a new day.

Moonbeam and I were skimming above a large body of water. The sun was on the horizon right over an emerging body of land. My forward vision was blinded, but looking down, we soon passed over a sandy beach and were in among palm trees. Moonbeam slowed her gait and landed. We were still just a shimmering mass. I looked behind us where the trees were casting long shadows, but saw none from us.

We must be in 1996, I thought, *but where?* The answer soon came to me when we approached the side of a busy highway. Although the cars were whizzing past, sleek-looking cars with very little chrome, I was able to see a Florida license plate. In fact, there were several Florida plates, confirming we must be in the Sunshine State. An overpass' green road sign indicated we were at the Gainesville exit number 382 on Interstate 75.

Moonbeam floated above the traffic and headed straight into the rising sun. When she came to rest, we were next to a parking area with half a dozen cars and trucks. Trees lined either side of a crushed-stone trail that stretched to the east. In the distance I could make out two people on bikes heading in our direction. *Why am I here?* I thought. *There are no Indians around, no soldiers, no teepees, nothing like our other trips. What does Teak-qua want me to see?*

We approached a sign at the beginning of the trail declaring it to be the Hawthorne State Rail Trail. The riders were drawing closer. I noticed that they were very close together. As they got within a quarter mile or so, I realized they were riding one bike, a bicycle built for two. There was a man on the front and a woman on the back. They were talking to each other, oblivious of the boy on horseback standing in front of them.

"Well, Dedra, aka Orangejewce2," the man said (referring to her chat-room name), "we made it."

"Yes, Maniac," she said (referring to his chat-room name), "we sure did. That was not a bad ride. How long was it?"

"About twenty-six miles, round trip. We made it in a little less than an hour and fifteen minutes. We averaged about twenty miles per hour."

"That's faster than I ever did it on my bike," she said.

"It's a flat route, and we did work together really well. How are you on liquids?"

"I could use some Gatorade. You got anymore?" she said taking off her gloves and helmet.

"Yeah, give me your bottle. The Gatorade's in the truck." She handed him a plastic water bottle. He got off the bike, and left her straddling it to keep it upright. I noticed there was no kickstand to support the bike if they both dismounted. He walked right through Moonbeam and me. It was just like our last trip when we rode transparently around the Indian village.

Bikes sure are fancy looking in 1996, I thought. *And they are wearing some strange-looking clothes and helmets.*

I turned to watch him as he opened the truck door, took out a bottle of greenish liquid, and poured it into her bottle. He then reached behind the seat of the truck and took out what looked like a pill and dropped it in with the liquid. He swirled the liquid as he walked back through us toward the woman. Handing her the bottle, she hopped off the bike while he held it. He guided the bike back toward the truck, as she walked through Moonbeam and me. She was drinking from the bottle. There was no visible evidence of the pill he put in it. Their shoes were making a clicking sound as they walked, as if they were in Holland, wearing wooden shoes and walking down a cobblestone path.

"Are you going to buy me breakfast?" she asked.

"Sure, as soon as you finish getting re-hydrated. Finish your Gatorade, while I put the tandem back on the truck. I know a little diner nearby that doesn't mind if we go in dressed like this." She took a long drink from the bottle, squirting all but a little of the liquid into her mouth.

"Whoa, I feel woozy," she said.

"Get in the truck and turn on the air-conditioning. You probably got a little dehydrated and overheated. You'll be all right in a minute." He finished lashing down the bike. The woman was now slumped down in the seat, but the man was not concerned. When he got in the driver's side, he hoisted her up and put a strap around her.

"There," he said. "The seat belt should keep you in place until we get back to the fifth wheel, after I return your helmet and bike clothes to your apartment." She moved slightly, but was clearly not in control.

What's a fifth wheel? I wondered. As the man drove off with the slumped-over woman in the seat beside him, Moonbeam started to trot. We got airborne in a few feet, and again the darkness appeared on the horizon. We were heading back into the black tunnel we left just minutes ago.

I started to ask myself if that was all of the future I was permitted to see. I wondered, *Who was the man?* and *Who was the woman?* and *What was in the bottle that made her pass out?*

As quickly as the tunnel appeared, it disappeared again, and we were near a mountaintop. There was a house at the top of the mountain, and a lot of snow. A strange-looking car or closed-in truck was approaching the top of the mountain. The vehicle had no problem in the heavy snow. It looked like some sort of futuristic Jeep, only a lot bigger and nicer. When the large Jeep got near the building, the garage door opened and it went in. The door immediately shut behind it. *Drat, I'll never find out who that was. Maybe I can look in the window.* "Moonbeam, can we get any closer?" Moonbeam did not give me her usual reassuring nod when I asked, but she did head in the direction of the house.

When we got closer, she slowed but did not detour from the beeline she was making for the side of the garage. I closed my eyes, and when I opened them, Moonbeam and I were standing in the garage. We had merely passed through the walls of the garage. The man was the same one we saw with the woman on the bike. He was taking the woman out of the large Jeep. She was naked except for her panties and a bra. He did not see us, for we were invisible. There was a door open to the house. Inside I could see a long corridor, and another open door near the end of it. I dismounted and followed the man as he carried the woman through the door. He kicked at the door to shut it. I started to get out of the swing of the door, but was too late. As if I were a puff of smoke, the door went right through me and slammed shut against the latch.

The man walked down the hall and into the other room. He closed the door behind him before I got there. I decided to continue to the end of the hall and see what was behind the door at the end.

Instead of opening the door, I tried walking straight through it, and did. In an instant, I was in the kitchen of the house.

"It would be nice to have some lights on," I said to myself. As if the house heard me, the lights in the kitchen came on. I heard the door open behind me, and in walked the man. I stood still, but he ignored me.

"That's strange," he said to himself. "I'll have to reprogram the computer to the pattern of my voice. Those lights should only come on when I tell them too." He gave a little shrug with his shoulders, dismissing whatever it was he was talking about.

He went to the refrigerator and took out a can of Budweiser, the same brand of beer my dad drank, only my dad had bottles, not cans.

"Lights off," he said, returning to the corridor. The lights went off, obeying his command. He closed the door behind him. I walked out of the kitchen and into what had to be the living room. From the glow of what looked like a television screen, I could see that it was a beautiful home. I noticed movement on the sofa and saw five cats lounging there, but they were alert and looking in my direction. Apparently they could see me or at least sensed my presence.

I'd like to afford a house like this someday, I thought.

"Lights on," I said. The lights turned on just as before. I had to admit my voice was similar to the man's. *I wonder what a computer is?* I thought, as I stared at the television that had only words on it, but they were in color.

Walking around the living room I saw some pictures on the wall near a built-in bookcase. When I got closer, I saw they were not pictures, but diplomas. They were engineering degrees from Ohio University and Texas A&M. I reached out to touch them, and drew near so I could read them.

I read out loud the larger of the two.

"To all to whom the presents may come greeting, be it known that...." I stopped reading when I saw the name. I looked at the smaller, Ohio University diploma, skipped down to "college of engineering and technology has conferred upon...."

The names on the documents were identical, not only to each other, but to my name as well. He even had the same middle name. Then it hit me. I realized that this must be me in the future. That is what Teak-qua cautioned me about. Returning to the kitchen area, I noticed a calendar on the wall. It was turned to January on the top and February on the bottom. The year was 1996.

"Lights off," I said as I walked in the same direction he went. The lights went out. I almost stepped on a cat, which was quizzically looking at me. *This is fun,* I thought as I sidestepped the cat. I walked through the kitchen door again and approached the door he had gone into earlier. There were no windows in the door, so I just walked right through it too. I found myself in a large, meat-cutting room. I knew that from my trips with my dad when he was a meat inspector. There was a difference, though; instead of a dead cow in the cutting room, the woman was, or what was left of her was, spread out on the stainless-steel table. I should say spread open on the table, for she was split open from her neck down. He was removing her internal organs. A radio was blaring something about a cheeseburger in paradise, by a singer I never heard before.

"What are you doing?" I blurted out, not thinking if he could hear me or not.

He heard something, but, after looking around, must have attributed the sound to the singer. He took a drink of the beer with his right hand. His left hand had a steel-mesh glove on it, which held parts of the body he was cutting with a large butcher knife. I had to get out of the room; the blood and guts were making me sick. When I turned, I almost stepped on another cat. I realized I did not have to sidestep it, but did so anyway. It was busy eating something. I looked closer and saw a heart. The heart, which must have been the woman's, was still beating as the cat bit into it. As I hurried through the door, he/I was singing loudly along with the song.

I felt weak as I got back on Moonbeam in the garage.

"Take me home, girl," I implored her. "And please make it as quick as possible. If this is me in the future and Teak-qua is right about not remembering this trip when I wake up, I want to forget this as soon as I can. What made me do that terrible thing to that beautiful woman?"

Two weeks later, it was the first day back at school. I remembered that I had a nightmare on my last night in the fort, but could not recall its content.

During those two weeks, my tunnel vision and the voice started. It came at night as I was trying to go to sleep. I would be lying in my bed, thinking about the events of the summer, when the voice that was my thoughts changed. It became loud and distant. At the same time, my vision would zoom as if looking through the wrong end of a pair of binoculars. It was almost as if my mind retreated to a far corner of the room, away from my physical being. My thoughts became the loud voice, but it was almost screaming at me, telling me what to do. I don't remember what it said exactly, but it berated me for the bad things I had done. I never mentioned my tunnel vision or the voice to anyone, for fear they might think I was crazy. Later in life I attributed it to growing pains, but still am not sure what it was.

Boo and I had gone our separate ways after our last encounter with Teak-qua. I went to see him once, but his mother could not find him.

"I'm sure he's around here somewhere," she said. "He was out playing with Bart in the backyard a little bit ago."

I found out later he was hiding in the coal bin because he thought he killed Bart. They had indeed been playing cowboys and Indians out behind Boo's house. Boo had a bow with rubber-tipped arrows, and Bart had Boo's BB gun. When Bart shot him in the shoulder, Boo busted the rubber tip off one of the arrows. He saw the top of Bart's head between the fork of two trees at the crest of a hill—the same hill I accidentally set on fire two years before, while playing with matches. Luckily a neighbor saw me while watering his yard and put the fire out. When my father got home from work, he told me he was going to burn all my fingers. He made me sit in my room and stare at a pack of matches for a long time before changing his mind.

When Boo let the arrow fly, it caught Bart in the exposed head. Boo went to investigate and saw Bart lying motionless at the bottom of the hill, an arrow stuck out of his head. When his father found him hiding in the coal bin, Boo told his father he killed Bart with an arrow.

A phone call to Bart's house found he had made it home on his own. Bart was alive and well, but with several stitches where the arrow went in and out of his scalp. Boo was thus confined to his house for a week, and his BB gun was taken away forever.

Bobbie-Lou quickly lost interest in me, since we did not invite her on another trip on Moonbeam. She was now "dating" David with his I'm-mister-cool, State Street Junior High, blue and gold jacket, and spit curls with the DA greased-up hair. I spent the time before the start of school replacing the screens in the windows of our house. That chore reminded me of how we helped Bobbie-Lou out of her window for her one and only trip back with us.

I saw Boo ride by the house several times in the last week before school started. He was with Skubini. We waved at each other, but did not stop and talk. I remembered the "trips" we took on Moonbeam and wondered if Boo did too. We never talked about it later in life, but I think he did remember.

Bobbie-Lou and I were now in junior high at State Street, but in different homerooms. My transition out of grade school was a turning point in my life. I was now officially a pre-teen and met a whole new batch of friends from other schools. Bobbie-Lou and I never talked again. Boo was still at South Liberty, and we did get together in the summers, but not like before.

Skubini was in the Catholic junior high school and went his separate way with new friends. He married his high school sweetheart, who was killed in a car wreck while he was in the army, waiting to go to Vietnam. We met occasionally when I was home on leave from the navy, but that was the extent of it.

David went into the army, after a failed attempt at college. I never saw him again. Linda moved to another state a year later.

My English class at State Street was my first period, in a different room from my homeroom. Going to a different room for each class was a new and unusual experience. I was excited and apprehensive at the same time.

"I want to find out how each of you writes," said Mrs. Williams. "Therefore, for tonight's assignment, I want you to write a two-hundred-word essay on how you spent your summer vacation." Groans went up from almost everyone in the room. I was silent, staring at the long, blond, and shiny hair of the girl in front of me. Penny, was someone who went to a different grade school, so we did not meet until junior high. She and her other grade school friends were thrown together with the rest of us from South Liberty. She was as pretty as Bobbie-Lou, whom I was fast forgetting.

"Today, we will learn the parts of speech," continued Mrs. Williams.

My mind suddenly connected to the assignment she had just given us. *How I spent my summer vacation,* I thought. *Teacher, you ain't gonna believe this.*

I got a C for grammar and spelling, but an A for imagination.

Epilogue

The tree I saw this morning formed an umbrella across the road.

It was reaching for the other side, another tree to hold.

Both the trees were young once; they grew so fast and full.

The one that stretched across the road finally reached its goal.

But, in taking so long to span the rift, the other had grown cold,

a rejection of the stretching one,

to leave it frail and old.

It was as if a love

had flourished,

to span between

two souls, and,

once they had

finally touched,

the other had

new goals. With

life almost at end,

it left the growing

one dismayed

to stand a short

while longer

with roots and

life decayed.

About The Author

Giovanni Andreazzi was born in Ohio, where, two weeks out of high school, he joined the United States Navy. He attended the Naval Academy and served aboard the submarine USS *Sam Houston*.

Following his military service, the author graduated from Ohio University and began a career with the Army Civil Service, obtaining a master's degree from Texas A&M and traveling the world. He has visited Russia, China, Japan, Singapore, Thailand, Hong Kong, Macao, South Korea, Finland, the Philippines, Sweden, Scotland, France, and Spain.

Before retiring, he worked as a project manager/engineer for the Indian Health Service, building, inspecting, and maintaining health facilities for Native Americans. The author of *Dedra* resides in Ohio, where he enjoys biking, weight lifting, cooking, and, of course, writing.

Printed in the United States
22993LVS00004B/115-381

9 781418 482510